Blood and Dominion

Evelyn Darrow

Copyright © 2024 by Evelyn Darrow

All rights reserved.

No portion of this book may be reproduced in any form without written permission from the publisher or author, except as permitted by U.S. copyright law.

Contents

1. Chapter 1 — 1
2. Chapter 2 — 10
3. Chapter 3 — 21
4. Chapter 4 — 28
5. Chapter 5 — 35
6. Chapter 6 — 40
7. Chapter 7 — 54
8. Chapter 8 — 69
9. Chapter 9 — 82
10. Chapter 10 — 91
11. Chapter 11 — 104
12. Chapter 12 — 115
13. Chapter 13 — 127
14. Chapter 14 — 145
15. Chapter 15 — 159
16. Chapter 16 — 173
17. Chapter 17 — 179

18.	Chapter 18	188
19.	Chapter 19	202
20.	Chapter 20	213
21.	Chapter 21	225
22.	Chapter 22	234
23.	Epilogue	251

Chapter 1

The most feared thing is death, unless you have a powerful queen with the word humanity word humanity almost stripped away from her.

"What day is it today?" She replied softly.

"It's Friday," the new maid's voiced out with a hint of fear.

"Ah, it is indeed today," she murmured, rising from her seat and studying herself in the mirror until she seemed concerned. "I seem to have gained some weight."

"No, you haven't," the maid hurriedly interjected, attempting to please her mistress.

"I have become fat," she insisted while still turning and studying herself, her tone sharp. At that moment, the maid sensed trouble brewing even though the Queen's expression was unreadable.

"Yes, perhaps you are correct," the maid cautiously conceded, her words hanging in the air before a sharp slap landed on her cheek.

With a wince, the maid nodded silently, her cheek stinging from the impact. She scrambled to her feet, casting a nervous glance towards her mistress, who had resumed her contemplation in the mirror. As the queen adjusted her gown, the room fell into a tense silence, broken only by the soft rustle of fabric. The maid dared not speak again, her heart pounding with anxiety. She knew all too well the consequences of displeasing the queen. Sera had already told her it was going to be hard to get used to the Queen's mood swings. She should be at least eighteen by now but still she was completely unpredictable.

"Next time, when I speak, provide only one response. I hate contradictions," she stated coldly, glaring down at her maid, who had already fallen to the ground.

A knock at the door saved the maid. "Your majesty?"

"What?" She snapped, a moment of silence followed until the voice at the door continued, "I see you are in a bad mood, again, should I come back later."

"Oh, it's you," she said, knowing exactly who that annoying person was, "Sera, you can come in."

As Sera entered the room, she wasn't shocked to see the new maid on the floor, it will be more shocking if the new maid doesn't quit by next week. "What happened?" she said as she quickly helped the terrified maid up from the floor.

"Well, you didn't train her well. I told her that I have gained weight and she lied to me," the queen explained.

Sera squinted, "Seriously, because of that?"

"So! Did I?" the queen enquired.

"No, you didn't. In fact, you have lost some weight," Sera replied nonchalantly. '

The queen smiled and added, "Yeah! That's why I like you. You see, new maid, that's how you answer my questions."

Sera continued trying to tease the Queen, "I still don't get it, with the amount of food and sleep you consume everyday you should be fatter than this but yet it feels like all that food goes into your attitude."

"Ha ha," she laughed sarcastically.

As the tension eased slightly in the room, the new maid, still trembling, cast a grateful glance towards Sera, who offered her a reassuring smile. "Thank you, Sera," she whispered, her voice barely audible.

Sera nodded in understanding before turning her attention back to the queen. "Your majesty, shall I prepare your tea as usual?"

The queen considered for a moment before looking knowing fairly that Sera won't agree to what she was about to request for."Sera, I want sweets this morning,"

"...," she remained silent on the queens requested.

"Please, Sera, just this once."

"Last time, I allow you to take sweets in the morn and you slept through the entire day, without doing any of your duties as a queen and now I should repeat that mistake again," Sera declared. "Unfortunately, You are getting tea whether you like it or not."

"Sera, if you don't allow me to take sweets, I am going to punish you," she declared.

"Hmm, Your majesty, I will assume you are just in a bad mood. I will get your tea ready."

"I hate you," the queen muttered, barely audible.

"I hate you, too," Sera replied with a smile followed by a slight bow before gliding out of the room, leaving the queen and the maid alone once again.

With Sera's departure, the room fell into a tense silence once more, though the atmosphere seemed slightly less stifling. The maid took a deep breath, her heart still racing from the encounter with the queen.

"You'll get used to her mood swings," she heard Sera's voice echoing in her mind. But as she glanced at the queen, who now seemed lost in thought, she couldn't help but wonder what other challenges lay ahead in her service to the queen.

As dawn broke over the kingdom, the weight of another demanding day settled upon the Queen's shoulders. Cloaked in a somber black gown adorned with stark white seams, her appearance alone commanded attention. With her hair woven into intricate braids, strands of white cascading like tendrils of frost, and lips painted a deep black, the Queen exuded an aura of mystery that captivated all who beheld her.

The anticipation in the court room was palpable as murmurs swirled amongst the courtiers, only to be silenced in an instant by the herald's announcement: "Her Majesty, the Queen." All eyes turned towards the throne as she made her entrance, her presence casting a spell of reverence and fear over the assembly.

Seated upon her throne, the Queen's piercing gaze swept over the gathered crowd before she delved into the stack of papers laid before her. A heavy sigh escaped her lips as she perused the troubling reports, her brow furrowing with concern. "Is it truly this bad?" she murmured, her voice cutting through the tense silence.

Her personal assistant, Adrian, nodded gravely. "I'm afraid so, Your Majesty. The situation is dire indeed."

The Queen's mind raced as she grappled with the implications of the kingdom's plummeting trade. How had this crisis unfolded under her watch? Questions buzzed like relentless insects in her mind, demanding answers that seemed elusive in the face of such adversity.

As the gravity of the situation sank in, a sense of urgency swept through the courtroom. The fate of the kingdom hung in the balance, and the Queen knew that decisive action would be required to restore order and salvage what remained of their reputation across the land.

"So, what do we do?" the Queen prompted, inviting the gathered courtiers to share their ideas. An elder ventured forth, suggesting a shift in trade focus. She narrowed her eyes slightly before motioning for him to continue. "Perhaps we could return to our traditional exports, starting with our prized dark woods," he proposed. The Queen's expression soured. "You suggest we barter our precious resources with those insatiable northerners? I am sorely disappointed, haven't you learnt anything," she lamented.

Another member of the court, previously silent, found the courage to speak up. "What if we invest in expertise to enhance the quality of our exports and seek counsel on revitalizing our domestic economy?"

The Queen fell silent, her expression inscrutable. Then, to everyone's surprise, a faint smirk graced her lips. "Well said. I am impressed today," she declared, causing a ripple of astonishment through the court. For once, no one faced her wrath, yet.

Turning her attention to the quiet courtier who had spoken up, the Queen inquired, "And what is your name?"

The person who spoke cleared their throat nervously before replying, "My name is Thomas, Your Majesty." The Queen nodded in acknowledgment. "Well, Thomas, your suggestion has merit. We shall explore the possibility of improving our exports with the help of experts. I have heard of these so-called Economic experts and even the King of the east has one under his rule" she declared, her tone softer than usual.

The courtiers and elders exchanged relieved glances, grateful for the Queen's unexpected leniency. Perhaps today wouldn't end in reprimands and punishments after all. "Thank you, Thomas," the Queen added with a slight smile, her demeanor momentarily easing the tension in the room. "Let us proceed with this plan and see where it takes us."

"Your majesty, those kinds of individuals are extremely expensive, especially those that are already working for another person," an elder added.

"Yes, but they certainly come at a price," she remarked casually, flipping through the papers in her hand. After hours of deliberation and strategizing, the Queen managed to grasp all the solutions at hand.

"Is there anything else?" she inquired, ready to adjourn the meeting. The court fell silent until another elder spoke up tentatively, catching her attention. "Your Majesty," he began hesitantly, "have you ever considered... having a king?"

The Queen's demeanor shifted, her expression hardening as she leaned back in her throne, fixing the elder with a piercing gaze. "And why would I do that?" she asked, her tone cool and composed.

The elder cleared his throat, sensing the tension in the air. "I don't mean to suggest that it's because you're a woman, Your Majesty," he hastened to explain. "But having a king could alleviate some of the burdens you bear and strengthen our kingdom's capabilities."

The Queen scoffed, a hint of frustration creeping into her voice. "So, because I'm a woman, I'm incapable of ruling alone?" she retorted, her eyes narrowing. "I assure you, I am more than capable of handling the responsibilities of this throne. When my mother ruled you didn't complain or do you want me to rule like her."

The courtiers exchanged uneasy glances, sensing the delicate nature of the conversation. The Queen's stance remained unwavering, her resolve unshaken by the elder's suggestion. She was determined to prove herself capable, regardless of the doubts cast upon her gender. Well, whatever they think of her she doesn't really have the energy to care.

The elder's suggestion lingered in the air, casting a shadow over the court. The Queen's gaze remained fixed on him, her expression steely and unwavering.

"Having a king," she began, her voice cutting through the silence like a blade, "implies that I am incapable of ruling this kingdom on my own. It suggests that my gender somehow diminishes my ability to govern effectively. Is that what you are entreating?" He couldn't utter another word because although it isn't reflecting on her face, she is on the verge of rage.

She rose from her throne, her presence commanding the attention of all who stood before her. "But let me be clear," she continued, her voice ringing with authority. "I am the Queen of this clan, and I answer to no one but myself. I have guided this kingdom through times of prosperity and adversity, and I will continue to do so with or without a king by my side."

The courtiers shifted uncomfortably under her piercing gaze, sensing the gravity of her words. The Queen's resolve was unyielding, her determination palpable in every syllable she spoke.

"I am more than capable of shouldering the burdens of leadership," she declared, her voice echoing throughout the chamber. "I do not need a king to validate my rule or lighten my load. I am perfectly capable of ruling alone."

The Queen's final statement hung in the air, a declaration of her unwavering independence and authority. Without another word, she turned on her heel and strode out of the court, her head held high and her demeanor unyielding.

The courtiers watched in stunned silence as the Queen departed, her departure signaling the end of the meeting. Left in her wake, they exchanged uneasy glances, grappling with the weight of her words and the power they held.

In the absence of their sovereign, the court dissolved into whispers and murmurs, each member contemplating the implications of the Queen's resolute stance. For in that moment, she had made it abundantly clear: she was a force to be reckoned with, a ruler who needed no one to validate her power or bolster her authority.

And as the echoes of her footsteps faded into the distance, the courtiers were left to ponder the true extent of the Queen's sovereignty, and the indomitable spirit that drove her reign. Nobody, even the Kings of the other lands feared her resolve.

Queen Ivana the Third

Chapter 2

"Your Majesty!" Sera's voice sliced through the queen's dreams like a sword, gently rousing her from her peaceful slumber. Waking the queen was like trying to convince a dragon to give up its hoard – a daunting task especially if that dragon is young.

"Ugh, leave me alone," the queen grumbled, clutching her pillow as if it were her last treasure. But Sera persisted, her urgency as persistent as a persistent salesperson trying to sell you something you don't need.

"Your Majesty, it's serious," Sera insisted, her tone a mixture of panic and determination. "We're talking end-of-the-world serious."

The queen groaned, pulling the covers over her head in a futile attempt to block out the impending doom. "Just give me five minutes... or ten," she pleaded, her voice muffled by the blankets.

"But Your Majesty, it's really, really bad," Sera persisted, her concern growing by the second. "Like, 'run-for-the-hills' bad."

Knowing she had to resort to drastic measures, she looked by the side in search of her secret weapon, when she finally found it, she smiled. Sera fetched a glass of water, carefully getting close to the queen to avoid her usual sudden burst of instinct and quickly poured it over the queen's head, eliciting a yelp of surprise from the drenched monarch.

"Sera!"

"Get up!"

"Sera, you're supposed to be my loyal subject, not my personal water assassin," the queen protested, glaring at her dripping attendant.

"It's ten o'clock, and something terrible has happened," Sera explained, her urgency undiminished by the queen's soggy state. "The only terrible thing happening right now is you ruining my beauty sleep," the queen retorted, attempting to salvage what was left of her dignity.

"Your Majesty, it's a declaration of war," Sera's voice cracked with concern, her words piercing through the queen's drowsy haze.

"From whom?" the queen replied casually, still trying to shake off the shock of being rudely awakened. She glanced down at her soaking nightgown, annoyance flickering in her eyes. "Did you really have to do that?"

"Because you're stubborn," Sera shot back, undeterred. "The king of the north has declared war on us."

The queen's frown deepened, her annoyance giving way to a sigh of resignation. "Kings," she muttered under her breath, shaking her head in exasperation.

With a sense of urgency, she leaped out of bed, her nightgown clinging to her like a wet blanket, and dashed out of the room without even bothering to change. After all, when war was at the gates, there was no time for proper attire, right? Or she was just too sleepy to think of that.

The sound of her footsteps echoed through the hallway as she followed Sera to the front of the courtyard. The tension in the air was palpable, with every person present trembling with fear at the ominous warning of impending danger. Their terror manifested in the form of the severed head of one of the elders, impaled on a stick and placed prominently in the center of the courtyard, when it was done nobody knew of it.

As the queen arrived, she showed no sign of concern. With a calm demeanor, she strolled into the courtyard, her expression unreadable. To the casual observer, it might have seemed as though she encountered such gruesome displays every day. But those who knew her best understood the truth – they knew what she had gone through to undergo such an impressive and yet disturbing demeanor.

Despite the gravity of the situation, the queen's nonchalant attitude seemed to have a calming effect on those around her. With her presence alone, she conveyed a sense of assurance and strength, reassuring her subjects that they would face this threat and undeterred by fear or intimidation.

"I see," she said nonchalantly, her voice betraying no hint of surprise or alarm. With measured steps, she approached the gruesome display of the decapitated head, her gaze unwavering.

"Your Majesty!" A messenger arrived at the scene, his expression fraught with anxiety. The queen tilted her head slightly, a small smile playing at the corners of her lips as she anticipated what he was about to say.

"Lemme guess, you also have bad news," she remarked, her tone laced with dry humor. The messenger's eyes widened in astonishment, taken aback by the queen's astuteness and seemingly unaffected demeanor in the face of such dire circumstances.

The messenger's voice echoed through the courtyard as he read aloud the message from the king of the east. "Your Majesty, I have decided to cut ties with your kingdom because our economy is not thriving under yours and we have found a better contract, thereby canceling our contract. But you being the queen I know you won't find this pleasing, but I invite you to my kingdom for compromise. I wish this doesn't cause an outburst of war between us" he recited, the words hanging heavy in the air. "His Majesty, King Charles of the East."

The queen stood in silence for a moment, her brow furrowing as she processed the unexpected news. The Kingdom of the east had been a valuable ally in times of war, their support instrumental in securing victories for her kingdom and theirs too. The sudden decision to sever ties left her feeling unsettled and perplexed, thinking he wouldn't usually do such stupid things when he knew exactly who the queen was.

"This is... unexpected," she finally spoke, her voice tinged with a hint of disbelief. Despite her surprise, she maintained her regal composure, and sighed.

An elder came and declared, "What do we do now? The queen was quiet for a moment still inspecting the head of one of the elders disgracefully placed in front of her. Irrespective of whosoever did this would pay for it whether they are powerful or not, she vowed quietly.

"This is the first elder," the queen declared and then looked at the elder who had stepped towards her, "you are the first elder now." The elder was shocked because he was not even in the level like the other elders to even contest for the first elder position. Elders were like the legislature of the kingdom; they made the laws and other decisions that merely required different points of views. Being a first elder makes you in charge of the legislature as the king of some sort and you have to be the second elder or third to get the first elder seat.

"Elder Thomas, what is your thought on that, " she said with a tilted head. He replied slowly and calmly because accepting this position might cause problems for him and maybe even his family, "Your majesty with all respect, I am not worthy of such a high position."

"That's too bad, I don't care what you think," she said nonchalantly. "First elder, prepare to leave for the Kingdom of the east, first thing tomorrow!" She declared as she turned and walked back into the castle as if nothing bad had happened. He bowed, and agreed but he knew his position was set, there was no changing her mind as she thinks of something.

The queen returned to her room, craving the comfort of her bed. With a contented sigh, she nestled into the soft pillows, ready to resume her slumber.

"Let's pick up where we left off," she mumbled to herself, sinking deeper into the covers. But before she could fully relax, a sharp knock at the door shattered the tranquility.

"Go away!" she snapped, her eyes heavy with sleep and irritation.

"I've come to help you get ready for the day," the new maid's voice quivered with fear.

"I said go away!" the queen repeated, her patience wearing thin.

Ignoring her command, the maid persisted, only to collapse to the floor in agony moments later. She couldn't believe what was happening because it felt like an invisible force clung to her as she became heavy all of a sudden, her body felt like it would break under such massive pressure. Sera, the queen's loyal attendant, rushed to her side, a mix of concern and resignation etched on her face.

"Not again," Sera muttered, realizing the queen's dark powers had struck once more, disrupting the peace and serenity of their morning routine.

Sera burst into the queen's room, her heart racing with urgency. The queen lay upon her bed, seemingly oblivious to the chaos unfolding around her, her expression serene as if a maid's life didn't hang in the balance.

"Your Majesty!" Sera's voice rang out, filled with desperation and frustration. "Stop it, you might kill her!"

But the queen remained unmoved, her focus fixed solely on reclaiming the interrupted slumber that eluded her grasp.

"If you don't stop," Sera threatened, her voice trembling with a mixture of fear and determination, "I will not make any dessert for you today, especially those cakes that you like."

A low growl escaped the queen's lips, a clear sign of her displeasure. Yet, to Sera's surprise, the new maid's convulsions seemed to ease slightly at the mention of withheld treats.

"Good girl," Sera cooed, her tone softening as she approached the sleepy queen. With swift movements, she gently removed the blanket and pillow, coaxing the queen to relinquish her hold on the coveted comfort of her bed.

"Leave me alone," the queen protested, clutching her pillow tightly to her chest.

"Let go, or you'll only eat vegetables for dinner," Sera retorted, her tone matter-of-fact as she stood her ground.

With a frustrated growl, the queen buried her face into the pillow, her anger palpable even as she knelt on the bed, glaring defiantly at Sera.

"Now, give me the pillow," Sera instructed, her voice firm yet gentle. After a tense standoff filled with glares and hisses, the queen reluctantly relinquished her grip on the pillow.

"Good girl," Sera praised softly, a hint of relief in her voice as she accepted the pillow. "Now, allow the new maid to help you take your bath, and I don't want to see any harm come to her again, ever!"

As the tension in the room eased slightly, Sera's gaze softened, a silent plea for cooperation and understanding passing between her and the queen.

The queen frowned as she reluctantly left her bed, her movements resembling those of a child being persuaded away from a playground. Each stomp of her feet conveyed her unhappiness to Sera, who sighed in understanding. Taking care of the queen was no easy task—she could be childish one moment and indifferent the next, but you won't blame her for that, she had her unfair share of child trauma. And her abilities as ruler of the demon clan only added to the challenge.

With an exasperated exhale, the queen emerged from the bathroom, her body still damp from the bath. The new maid, following closely behind, gently suggested, "Your Majesty, won't you at least dry your hair?"

"Who cares?" the queen replied dismissively, her frustration evident in her tone. "I'll dry eventually. Let me enjoy myself since I can't even enjoy my sleep anymore," she added, casting a glance at Sera.

With a resigned nod, Sera conceded, understanding that sometimes it was best to prioritize the queen's wishes to avoid further conflict. In the realm of the demon clan, diplomacy and deference were crucial, even in the face of the queen's whims.

"You can go," Sera instructed the new maid, who bowed respectfully and exited the room. Sera then fetched a comb and a dry towel, positioning a chair near the mirror. However, the queen shook her head in disagreement, folding her arms across her chest.

"Do you want your hair to start to smell?" Sera inquired, raising an eyebrow in concern.

"Let it smell. If I wish, I could go and attend to my queenly duties like this," the queen retorted, her tone defiant. "Naked!"

Sera's eyes widened in disbelief. "Please, I think you've had too much to drink. Come, let me get you ready." Despite Sera's urging, the queen remained reluctant, keeping her distance from Sera. She couldn't comprehend why she couldn't simply dress casually for the day.

"Ivana the third!" Sera's voice rang out, startling the queen. It was a name she had forbidden anyone to utter, and the mention of it sent a shiver down her spine. Nobody knew why, well only few, but it seemed to be connected to her late mother, Queen Ivana the second.

The queen remained silent, her arms hanging limply at her sides, as if stung by a painful memory. Sera quickly realized her mistake and rushed to apologize, approaching the queen cautiously and guiding her to the dressing mirror.

Whenever her full title was spoken, the queen's emotions would often spiral into anger or sadness, a testament to the deep-seated pain she carried within.

After several minutes of dressing, the queen was nearly ready, with only her hair remaining undone. "Ah!" she cried out in frustration as the comb snagged in her hair once again.

"Stay still. Don't you know your hair is tough?" Sera replied, her hands still working through the tangles. Everything about Ivana seemed resilient, even her hair.

"My hair is not tough, it's just not cooperating today," the queen retorted.

"Nope, your hair is worse than heartbreak," Sera quipped back.

"And how is that supposed to be?" the queen questioned, her curiosity piqued despite her irritation.

"Have you ever fallen in love before?" Sera's question hung in the air, laced with curiosity and concern.

The queen's response was swift, a dismissive scoff accompanied by a steely glare. "Love," she echoed, her tone sharp with defiance. "The only thing I love is my sleep."

Sera paused, her gaze unwavering as she observed the queen's hardened expression. But beneath the facade of strength, Sera sensed a hint of vulnerability, a flicker of loneliness hidden behind the queen's icy demeanor, it was there — somewhere.

"Your Majesty," Sera spoke softly, her words carefully chosen. "I understand your reluctance, but closing yourself off to love may only lead to solitude. Even though you are more than capable of ruling the kingdom alone, it doesn't mean you have to do it alone. I heard what happened in the courtroom the other day."

The queen's eyes narrowed slightly, her guard momentarily slipping as Sera's words struck a chord within her. For a fleeting moment, the weight of responsibility seemed to press down upon her shoulders, the burden of solitude looming large in her mind.

"I don't need anyone," the queen asserted, her voice firm but tinged with uncertainty.

Sera's gaze softened, a gentle reassurance in her eyes. "Perhaps not, Your Majesty, but companionship can bring warmth to even the coldest of hearts."

The queen remained silent, her thoughts drifting to the vast expanse of her kingdom and the countless souls she ruled. Was it truly possible to rule with an iron fist and a heart of stone? Or was there room for something more amidst the shadows of power?

As the weight of her crown bore down upon her, the queen's resolve wavered, a seed of doubt planted by Sera's words. Perhaps, just perhaps, there was room for love in the heart of a queen, but still she doesn't really feel like she needs any of those, right now.

Chapter 3

It was yet another day, shrouded in the cloak of uncertainty. Outside, the sky stretched wide and clear, the sun casting its golden rays through the billowing curtains of her chamber. Yet within, the queen lay ensconced in the embrace of sleep, her slumber uninterrupted by the cares of the world, the most peaceful time of the day for her.

For Queen Ivana, sleep was a sanctuary, a refuge from the demands of ruling her kingdom. Some might question how she could rule effectively when she cherished her rest above all else. But to Ivana, she can't explain why once she touches her bed it's just irresistible to leave it, unless some annoying someone, comes along.

As the sunlight danced upon her peaceful form, one could almost envy the peace that enveloped her. How could one so deeply immersed in the world of dreams wield the scepter of power? Yet those who knew her understood that behind closed eyes lay a mind sharp and astute, capable of navigating the most treacherous of political waters.

In the quiet tranquility of her chamber, Queen Ivana still reigned supreme, her kingdom bending to her will even in the depths of her slumber. She doesn't even flick a finger for everything to run smoothly in her clan.

"Your Majesty! Wake up!" A voice called out, but there was no response. "For God's sake, why do you always make me do this, every morning?" Sera added with a hint of frustration. A low groan escaped the queen as she shifted away from Sera's voice. "Please, come back in the next hour."

"Your Majesty, you have to visit the King of the East today—remember!" Sera urged, emphasizing the importance of the queen's impending task.

"I've changed my mind; we'll go next week," the queen replied, her voice muffled by the plushness of her bedding. She seemed to sink even deeper into the comfort of her bed, showing no sign of urgency.

"Look, you're the queen—many look up to you. Isn't it a pity that you can't even try to be punctual?" Sera declared, her frustration evident in her tone. But the queen only groaned in response, determined to continue her slumber as she clutched her pillow the more, hoping that she would just go away.

Sera glanced at her mistress, pondering once again the strange characters of the queen. Beyond her formidable abilities, this penchant for rest seemed almost like a sickness—an anomaly in the common royal duties. She is full of contradictions and yet, she hates it when anyone does it to her, the irony is quite frustrating. It's quite difficult to unravel the mysteries of the queen, nobody can, she won't allow it.

"I will get the water again," Sera threatened, her tone firm.

"Sera, we may be friends, but if you dare sprinkle water on me, I will burn your intestines and blood will flow through your eyes—literally," the queen replied, her threat delivered with a casual nonchalance. Yet, to Sera, it held a little weight of danger, even though she is the closest to her. Although the queen could be a little amiable to all, crossing her could unleash a wrath as fierce as the fires of hell. Her threats, even the casual ones, were not to be taken lightly.

Sera stood still, watching her beloved queen choose sleep over her duties once again, knowing that to challenge her further would be to invite consequences she dared not face. Not now at least, she has her ways to keep the queen in check.

Sera continued to contemplate, her mind racing with ideas on how to rouse the queen from her slumber. "Hmm," she murmured to herself, lost in thought.

"What?" The queen's curiosity was piqued by Sera's contemplative tone.

"Ah, nothing," Sera replied hastily, realizing she had been caught in her reverie.

The queen turned and opened one eye, fixing Sera with a curious gaze. "Seriously, if you don't have anything important, please go," she urged, her patience wearing thin.

"Well..." Sera began slowly, hoping to capture the attention of the sleepy queen, "my spy has returned, and he's brought some news."

The queen merely hissed in response, seemingly intent on returning to her slumber. Undeterred, Sera pressed on.

"According to him, they've found an expert who may be able to help our economy. He's said to be the best in his country."

She remained unmoved desperately trying to return to sleep. "And look at the bright side, if you get him early now, he will tackle economic issues with advanced knowledge, which implies that you will get more time to...., sleep!" Sera added stressing the last word.

These words stirred the queen from her drowsiness. Getting more sleep is important, so it's just a little sacrifice to ensure more sleep, prompting her to spring out of bed and move to the window. Gazing out at the colorful garden below, a hint of irritation crossed her features. "Sera, you've disturbed me enough. I can't sleep anymore. You've won, be happy," she grumbled as she turned her head towards Sera with a nonchalant look.

A smile tugged at Sera's lips at the queen's begrudging acceptance of defeat. "Well, actually, it's my job to disturb you, remember? But in all seriousness, we have found an expert."

"Then why are you disturbing me? If you think he or she is great, then hire them," the queen entreated, making her way back to her bed and slowly crawling back into it.

Sera cleared her throat to regain the queen's attention. "But the problem is that he rejects offers from anybody of nobility, irrespective of the amount of money," she explained.

The queen furrowed her brow in thought. "So how is that a problem?" she inquired, puzzled by Sera's concern.

"Well, he's more likely to reject the offer to come here to work for us, especially considering how nearly everyone fears the Demon Clan," Sera added, her voice tinged with concern.

The queen pondered Sera's words, recognizing the wisdom in her concern. Indeed, the mere mention of the Demon Clan often raised red flags and evoked distrust among outsiders. Their reputation preceded them, making it challenging to gain the trust and cooperation of others.

The queen sighed, acknowledging the validity of Sera's point. The stigma surrounding the Demon Clan was a constant obstacle in their efforts to forge alliances and garner support for their kingdom, not like they completely needed them. It was a burden she bore, knowing that their reputation often overshadowed their true intentions.

"True," the queen conceded, her expression reflecting the weight of their predicament. "But still this is an opportunity to change perceptions. If we can convince this expert to work with us, it could demonstrate to others that the Demon Clan is capable of positive change."

Sera nodded in agreement, encouraged by the queen's optimism. "Yes, you're right, Your Majesty. This could be a chance to show the world that we're not defined by our past, since this is our goal to make the demon clan better, after what she did." Sera hinted out only to be met by a sudden change in the Queen's face, as she sighed.

"Her!"

A sudden silence fell as Sera contemplated whether it was right to have brought out such sensitive matter. Something that was best left in the past.

"So now, I have to travel to the east, such a long journey." she sighed. A smiled knowing fairly that the queen hates traveling about especially to those far lands but she had to do it. "Don't worry, I will also follow you. With me, time will fly, well, that is if you don't fall asleep through the entire journey." Her words were met with a scoff from the queen.

With renewed determination, the queen resolved to pursue this opportunity, determined to prove that the Demon Clan was deserving of trust and respect. It would be a challenging endeavor, but one she was willing to undertake for the betterment of her kingdom.

"Alright, let me just sleep a little bit," the queen murmured, slowly pulling her beddings around her, since Sera had taken her blanket.

"Your Majesty! There is no time, stop this," Sera exclaimed, her voice filled with concern. The urgency of their situation weighed heavily on her, and she knew they couldn't afford to waste any more time.

The queen paused, her eyes meeting Sera's with a mixture of irritation and exhaustion. Yet, beneath the weariness, a spark of determination flickered. She knew Sera was right—they couldn't afford to delay any longer.

With a resigned sigh, the queen pushed herself up from the bed, casting one last longing glance at the warmth of her covers. "Fine," she relented, her voice tinged with reluctance. "Let's go."

Sera nodded in satisfaction, relieved that her words had finally penetrated the queen's stubbornness. They left the chamber's comforts and ventured out into the unknown world beyond, where challenges awaited and alliances needed to be formed.

Chapter 4

The world was divided into four kingdoms, each based on the cardinal points. Within each kingdom, numerous clans thrived, each claiming their own portion of the land. Among them, the Kingdom of the East stood out as the third most powerful, its king rumored to have forged an alliance with the feared Demon Clan, which was quite unexpected.

This seemingly simple alliance, however, had far-reaching consequences. The mere association with the Demon Clan made the King of the East a target for the most powerful kingdoms. You might wonder why such an alliance would provoke such hostility. The answer lies in the reputation of Queen Ivana.

Queen Ivana, ruler of the Demon Clan, was known for her perplexing and formidable nature. Her name alone struck fear into the hearts of many, and her influence spread far beyond the borders of her own clan, even though they were just a mere clan in the south. Any kingdom or ruler associated with her was viewed with suspicion and often targeted by those seeking to maintain their own power.

In this tense landscape, the King of the East found himself walking a precarious tightrope, balancing alliances and rivalries while navigating the shadow cast by the Queen's reputation. Although they were rivals, they didn't cause trouble to the East because of the queen, but for this sudden change, it raises red flags.

"What are you thinking of?" Sera questioned, observing her mistress lost in thought as she gazed through the carriage window. They had been on the road for almost a week now, traveling towards their destination.

The queen snapped back to reality at Sera's inquiry. "What?" she responded, momentarily disoriented. "What were you thinking of?"

"Oh!" she exclaimed, settling back into her seat. "I still don't understand why the Kingdom of the East did ally with us, considering our bad reputation and their own considerable power." Sera couldn't help but smile. "Hmm, maybe he likes you."

The queen fixed Sera with a piercing stare. "Does it look like I'm joking?" she retorted sharply, her tone laced with irritation.

"No, no, I was just saying, but it is indeed plausible, you know. Men often help women they like," Sera continued, trying to diffuse the tension. "Seriously, what do you have against them?"

The queen scoffed, shaking her head. "I don't have anything against them."

"But yes, you are right," Sera replied, steering the conversation back to the original topic. "Why would the mighty king of the East ally with us, only to later cancel the alliance?" The queen fell silent, lost in thought. After a moment, she added, "Am I an evil person?"

Sera's eyebrows furrowed with concern. "No, Your Majesty," she reassured. "You're just misunderstood. Your methods may be unconventional, but your intentions are always for the good of our clan."

"That's not the answer I wanted to hear," she said nonchalantly.

The Queen's words hung in the air, her dissatisfaction palpable. Sera hesitated, unsure of how to respond. After a moment, she gathered her thoughts and spoke carefully.

"I understand, Your Majesty," Sera began, her tone gentle yet firm. "But perhaps the answer you seek lies not in the opinions of others, but in your own actions and intentions."

The queen regarded Sera thoughtfully, her expression softened by her advisor's words. After a brief pause, she nodded slowly, a flicker of resolve in her eyes. But then, she added with a hint of frustration, "I hate contradictions."

She remained silent, understanding the queen's aversion to contradictory statements, although her majesty is entirely a walking contradiction. Instead, she simply nodded in acknowledgment, allowing the weight of the queen's declaration to linger in the air between them.

The journey to the Kingdom of the East stretched on for almost two weeks, punctuated by stops in passing villages and towns along the way. Finally, they arrived at the kingdom's gate, boldly emblazoned with the words, 'East Kingdom.'

However, this gate was merely the entrance to the kingdom, not the actual palace of the king. The palace lay deep within the kingdom itself, requiring another week's journey to reach its hallowed halls.

"Ah, yes, we have finally arrived," Sera exclaimed, her excitement met with the queen's persistent slumber. Sera couldn't help but marvel at the queen's ability to sleep anywhere, even in the carriages. "She must be exhausted," Sera mused to herself as she disembarked from the carriage, greeted by the king's personal assistant, Philip.

"We've been awaiting your arrival ever since we heard of your visit," Philip remarked, motioning for the servants to retrieve their luggage. "It's been quite some time, Philip," Sera responded warmly. "Well, messages tend to travel slowly from the far south," Philip explained. Then, his gaze turned inquiringly towards Sera. "But where is the queen?"

Sera sighed, "She's still asleep." Philip's eyebrows shot up in surprise. "Where is she?" he inquired. Sera turned and gestured towards the carriage. Philip's eyes widened further. "Really? Shouldn't you wake her?" he asked, a hint of concern in his voice.

Almost panicking, Sera replied, "I dare not, again. She's quite obsessed with her sleep, you know." She glanced back at the carriage before continuing, "And you're aware of how impulsive she can be."

Philip nodded knowingly. "Of course, I remember. Our enemies are still recovering from the damage she inflicted upon them." Sera sighed and added, "If only she weren't so unpredictable and obscure."

"Indeed," Philip agreed.

"What are you guys whispering about?" Queen Ivana interrupted with a yawn, her arms stretched dramatically as if rehearsing for a play. Sera jumped in surprise at her sudden wakefulness.

"Your Majesty!" Philip's formality clashed with the queen's disheveled appearance.

"Yes, Philip, I need a bed," the queen announced, as if she had just uncovered a groundbreaking revelation. Sera couldn't help but roll her eyes.

"Seriously, Your Majesty, you just woke up from a nap in the carriage," Sera retorted, unable to hide her exasperation.

"I need a bed, do I need to spell it out for you?" the queen insisted, her yawn turning into a theatrical gesture.

"My apologies, Your Majesty. Right this way," Philip replied, trying to maintain his composure amidst the queen's morning antics.

With a dramatic wave, Queen Ivana followed Philip, her entourage trailing behind. As they entered the palace, Sera couldn't help but chuckle at the queen's unique way of starting the day.

"Your Majesty, you never fail to entertain," Sera commented with a grin.

The queen turned to her with a mischievous twinkle in her eye. "Life's too short to be serious all the time, Sera. Now, let's see if they have a bed fit for a queen!"

And with that, they disappeared into the grandeur of the palace, leaving behind a trail of laughter and lightheartedness.

Some moments later.

"Argh!" She groaned, trying to find a comfortable position on the bed. "Even their bed is not comfortable." Sera just scoffed and continued unpacking her mistress's clothes.

"Sera!" She yelled. "Yes, your majesty! No need to yell, I am here," Sera replied calmly. "I can't sleep," she added, folding her arms while sitting on the bed. "Well, that's the consequence of sleeping for more than eight hours."

"What?... No, I didn't sleep that long."

Sera just smiled, "Hmm, you are truly strange. They actually postponed the meeting because you were sleeping three hours ago," Sera emphasized the last words. Surprisingly, Ivana was unmoved as she slowly grew quiet and replied, "I actually have a bad feeling about this place."

"What do you mean?" Sera questioned. "I can't actually tell, but I am sensing something dark." "Are you sure you're not sensing yourself?" Sera teased. Ivana scoffed, "I know my own aura, but this thing is different." Sera continued, "Well, whatever it is, I hope we won't be involved."

"I hope," she said, getting lost in her thoughts as usual.

As the silence settled between them, the air in the room seemed to grow heavier, laden with unseen tension. Ivana's mind wandered, contemplating the new ominous feeling that lingered in the air. Despite the brightness of the sun outside, a shadow seemed to loom over her thoughts, casting doubt and unease over her mind.

Sera watched her young queen carefully, sensing the shift in her demeanor. She knew better than to dismiss Ivana's instincts; after all, the queen's intuition had saved them from countless dangers in the past. With a furrowed brow, Sera pondered the implications of Ivana's dreadful feeling, wondering what darkness lay ahead.

And amidst it all, the queen couldn't shake the feeling that they were teetering on the edge of something dark.

Chapter 5

The courtroom buzzed with anticipation as the renowned queen of the demon clan, Queen Ivana, made her grand entrance, fashionably late as usual. Her elegant stride commanded attention as she gracefully took her seat, trailed by a servant.

As the members gathered, the King of the East rose to address the assembly, offering a surprising gesture of gratitude to Queen Ivana. His unexpected bow stirred murmurs among the courtiers, prompting the king to justify his actions by acknowledging Queen Ivana's crucial assistance during difficult times.

Acknowledging the tension in the room, he emphasized the significance of the demon clan's alliance, regardless of its size. With the looming threat of inflation and frequent attacks, the kingdom faced dire economic challenges, underscoring the importance of unity and cooperation among the kingdoms.

"I summon Kyson, our esteemed royal economic expert," the king declared.

Promptly, a distinguished man emerged, striding confidently across the courtroom with a regal air. Beside him, a young assistant trailed with a large rolled-up parchment—likely his aide.

"Kyson, what is the state of our economy?" the king inquired.

"Your Highness," Kyson bowed respectfully, "the economy teeters on the edge of uncertainty. However, before I proceed, I must express gratitude to her Majesty, the Queen of the mysterious demon clan, for her invaluable assistance despite the pressures she faces."

Instantly, a twinge pricked her mind, a sensation that often alarms impending trouble.

Kyson pressed on, "Unfortunately, the aftermath of the wars has only compounded our challenges. The latest report indicates that our alliance with the demon clan benefits only the smaller factions. Our key trading partners are concerned about dealing with us due to their fear of the demon clan."

Sera, who observed the proceedings, sensed that the queen might soon lose her temper if things continued in this manner.

"What exactly are you suggesting?" Sera interjected, unable to contain herself. Kyson, visibly irritated by Sera's audacity, glanced down at her with disdain.

"And who granted you the authority to address me?" he retorted.

"It was a straightforward question. I believe we need clarification on your explanation," Sera replied confidently.

Kyson huffed in annoyance. "Allow me to simplify it for you. Our kingdom's reputation has suffered due to our association with the demon clan."

The courtroom buzzed with disbelief as Kyson's words hung in the air, directed straight at the demon queen. Sera, now on the offensive, voiced what everyone was thinking.

"So, you're blaming us for the decline of your economy, is that it?" Sera's tone was sharp, her eyes flashing with defiance.

Kyson paused, considering his next words carefully. "Indeed, but there is a solution that could benefit us all," he finally offered, drawing the attention of the entire court.

"As you are aware, alliances by contract are fragile and can be terminated at any moment. However, alliances by marriage offer a more enduring solution," Kyson revealed, his voice filled with conviction.

Sera's heart raced as she turned to her mistress, who remained composed, seemingly unfazed by Kyson's proposal. "Marriage?" Sera's voice wavered with disbelief.

The courtroom fell silent, awaiting the queen's response. After a moment, Kyson continued, his voice steady and measured. "Indeed, a marriage has the potential to unite not just individuals, but entire nations and worlds. Because once we are united in marriage the entire world will see that the demon clan has become a real part of the East Kingdom. However..." His words trailed off as Sera cut in, her frustration palpable. "There it is!"

Kyson raised an eyebrow, surprised by Sera's interruption. "Yes, however..." he continued, "such a union must be carefully considered and approached with caution. It requires the agreement and commitment of both parties involved."

The tension in the room thickened as Kyson's words hung in the air. Sera glanced at her queen, who remained deep in thought, her expression unreadable. It seemed like she wasn't even concentrating on what was happening.

Finally, after a moment of silence, the queen spoke, her voice commanding yet tinged with uncertainty. "Continue," she instructed Kyson, her gaze fixed on him with an intensity that made even him falter for a moment.

Kyson cleared his throat and proceeded to outline the details of his proposal, but Sera couldn't shake the feeling of unease settling in the pit of her stomach.

"But... the demon clan joining the East Kingdom as one?" Every member of the demon clan present was enraged by this proposal, and the courtroom erupted into noise. Sera watched the queen, who seemed unfazed; instead, she was focused on the young man standing close to Kyson.

"That will be all, Kyson," the king interjected, attempting to diffuse the tension. "Your Majesty, there's no need to rush into this matter. Take your time."

Ivana chuckled softly as a grim tugged her lip. "Let me get this straight. If I marry you, the alliance remains, but my clan is lost. But if I don't..."

"Then you'll be considered an enemy. This is a new era; there's no room for indecision or lukewarm," Kyson calmly added. From that moment on, the queen lost interest in the discussion. "Alright, I guess I should be leaving."

With a calm demeanor, Ivana rose from her seat. Kyson was taken aback by the queen's audacity to reject the King of the East. After all, her kingdom was just a small clan in the far south, who cares about their reputation. She left the courtroom without looking back, her defiance leaving an impression. As for the king, he couldn't help but admire the queen's strength — a woman with true power indeed! And still he doesn't know why he is so obsessed with her.

Later on, as the queen drifted into a restless slumber, Sera couldn't shake off the unsettling feeling in her gut. She knew there was more to the king's proposal than met the eye, and the consequences of rejecting it could be significant. And yet, seeing the queen sleeping quiet, peaceful and untroubled, it makes her feel a bit of relief but still, why?

Chapter 6

The sun shone brightly as it climbed higher in the sky, casting a warm glow over the morning grass and making the flowers in the garden bloom in vibrant hues. The garden's beauty complemented the palace's impressive architectural design. Workers and servants bustled about, while guards patrolled the grounds. Sunlight streamed through the elegant curtains of a room adorned with luxurious furnishings. The wooden floors, made from the finest oak, gleamed under the morning light, and the carefully chosen furniture matched the intricate design of the curtains and bed.

Despite the grandeur surrounding her, the queen lay restless on her grand bed, tossing and turning. Her discomfort was evident as she shifted from side to side, disturbing the otherwise serene atmosphere. Her sudden movements startled Sera, who was already in the room, meticulously preparing everything the queen would need for the day.

"What...?" the queen mumbled, her surprise evident as she glanced at Sera, whose face was a mixture of concern and mild shock.

"Oh," Sera began, her expression softening. "I thought you were having one of those episodes again. I wouldn't want a repeat of the chaos we had back at the clan."

The queen squinted at Sera, still puzzled. Despite understanding the reference, she wondered why Sera would think such things, especially in the morning.

Sera sighed and held out a small mirror. "Take a look," she said, her tone gentle but firm.

The queen took the mirror, her brow furrowing in confusion. As she glanced into it, her expression turned cold. Her face had gone pale, and dark veins had appeared, stretching from her neck up to her face. The veins were clearly visible, pulsating with a faint, dark glow that seemed otherworldly.

The queen slowly lowered the mirror, her gaze drifting to the ceiling. This phenomenon was familiar, but its sudden appearance was unsettling. It signaled a potential threat lurking around the palace.

"I saw you were restless," Sera said, trying to divert the queen's focus.

"Something, somewhere," the queen muttered, her tone contemplative.

"Like I said before, are you sure you're not sensing yourself? Besides, you're the only one with such dark energy," Sera said with a touch of humor.

The queen pouted. "Sera, I want to go back. I'm bored with this Eastern palace, and their bed here is uncomfortable."

Sera raised an eyebrow, surprised by the sudden change in mood. "We arrived just yesterday. And don't forget, we need to find that expert."

The queen growled at the reminder of their mission.

"I know Kyson will never agree, and besides I know you might hate him —." The queen tilted her head as she looked straight at Sera, the looks in her eyes reminding her that she only hated only one person, Sera cleared her throat, cutting her off. "Of course, we could try to get his assistant, Alex. He's been with Kyson for a long time. When I asked him to join us yesterday, he turned us down, even with the promise of triple his fee. He seemed to dislike us, so I'm not sure if there's anything more we can do."

The queen's eyes glinted mischievously. "Well, there is always abduction."

Sera's eyes widened. "No, absolutely not!"

"So then what do you suggest? I can't use my powers to change his mind. But I could force him, which is a quicker solution."

"You're a beautiful woman," Sera began.

"No!"

"You're a beautiful woman. Your face is pretty, your hair is gorgeous, and the look in your eyes could charm any man. Let's not even talk about —"

"Sera!"

"What I'm saying is you should try to talk to him. You might have a better chance of convincing him. Although your attitude can be a bit tough, I think you could manage."

"I am not talking to anyone," the queen said firmly.

Sera smiled as she carried a small bowl of sweets and tasty-looking biscuits. The treats were perfectly browned, their sugar coating sparkling in the sunlight and emitting a tantalizing aroma.

"Sera, where are you going?" the queen asked, watching as Sera prepared to leave.

"I have other tasks to attend to," Sera said as she turned the door knob. The soft clicks of the knob reminded her that she was about to leave with sweets.

"Sera, the sweets."

"Oh, these?" Sera replied, leaving the door half open. "These are meant for you..."

"Okay, then give them to me," the queen interrupted, her eyes fixed on the bowl.

"Meant for you, when you go and talk to him," Sera added.

The queen's eyes narrowed. "How dare you?"

"It's simple. Agree to go and meet him, and you get these."

After some hissing and a persistent stare at Sera, the queen finally muttered, "Fine!"

Sera's smile widened as she placed the bowl on a side table next to the bed. "You'll find him at the workers' quarters. They said he usually works around the place in the mornings."

As Sera walked to the door, she glanced back to see the queen staring intently at the bowl of sweets. The queen had always had a sweet tooth, even if she pretended otherwise.

With a final nod, Sera closed the door, leaving the queen to contemplate her impending meeting, her gaze lingering on the delicious treats.

The queen strode through the palace corridors with an air of unapproachable authority. Every step she took drew the eyes of servants and guards, their gazes a mix of awe and apprehension. Her commanding presence left no doubt about her status, and the subdued whispering that followed in her wake only underscored her significance.

Arriving at the workers' quarters, the queen's entrance was met with stunned silence. The workers, momentarily halted in their tasks, looked up with wide eyes as she approached. The room fell into a hushed reverence, their attempts at politeness palpable in the nervous greetings they offered.

The queen's gaze swept over them with cold detachment. "I don't need your politeness," she said with a voice that cut through the air like a blade. "I'm looking for Alex."

A ripple of concern spread among the workers. One of them, a man with a wary expression, stepped forward. "Your Majesty, I'm afraid you've just missed him. He left for another duty, though we don't know where he's gone."

The queen's face remained impassive, but her eyes betrayed a glimmer of frustration. She had hoped to find Alex and resolve her concerns directly. Now, with no immediate way of locating him and no intention of returning to the palace where Sera would undoubtedly insist on her rest, she faced a dilemma.

With a sigh, the queen decided against returning to the palace. Sera would never allow her to rest, and she needed a distraction from the oppressive sense of dark energy that had been troubling her. Her thoughts briefly wandered, and she made up her mind to explore the town. Perhaps a change of scenery might ease her troubled mind, even if only momentarily.

The queen left the workers' quarters and made her way out of the palace.

As she stepped onto the cobblestone streets, the lively atmosphere of the town enveloped her. The market was bustling with activity; vendors called out their wares, children darted between stalls, and the aroma of fresh bread and spices mingled in the air.

The queen wandered through the market, her keen eyes taking in the colorful displays and the animated interactions of the townsfolk. She paused at various stalls, her gaze lingering on the diverse array of goods—bright fabrics, intricate jewelry, and exotic spices, her simple attire disguised her royal status, allowing her to blend in with the common folk. . Each new sight and sound served as a temporary distraction, pulling her focus away from the unsettling darkness she had felt earlier.

The queen continued her exploration, moving through the town with a sense of purpose. The lively environment provided a brief respite from her internal turmoil, and she hoped that immersing herself in the town's energy would offer some relief. For now, she was content to let the world outside the palace walls occupy her mind, if only for a little while

Her eyes sparkled with childlike wonder as she explored the vibrant marketplace, taking in the sights and sounds of the east kingdom. The colorful displays of goods and the chatter of merchants filled the air, a sharp contrast to courtly affairs.

Amidst the array of shops, her gaze was drawn to a glittering necklace displayed in a storefront window. Its shimmering look caught the sunlight, casting a mesmerizing glow that seemed to beckon to her. Intrigued, she approached the shop, her curiosity piqued by the allure of the exquisite adornment.

The necklace was simple yet irresistible, its sparkling surface casting a spell over Queen Ivana. Lost in admiration, she reached out to touch it, only to be jolted back to reality by the shopkeeper's reminder that she hadn't paid.

Flushed with embarrassment, Ivana realized she had no money with her. Unused to the mundane task of purchasing goods, she felt a pang of frustration at her oversight. If this was her clan she could get anything without thinking of the payment.

The tension in the air was palpable as the shopkeeper's gaze bore down on her, and Ivana could feel the curious stares of onlookers as they began to gather around.

Just when it seemed her predicament would escalate into a scene, a young man appeared at her side, offering to pay for the necklace. Relief flooded through Ivana as she accepted his kind gesture, grateful for his intervention.

He took the necklace from the shopkeeper, only to turn and find Queen Ivana scrutinizing him with a critical eye. "Is everything alright?" he asked, a hint of nervousness creeping into his voice.

"Oh, sorry! You remind me of someone," she declared, her tone distant. "Well, I hope I don't remind you of someone bad," he quipped, attempting to lighten the mood, but the queen remained unaffected.

He had the average appearance of a commoner: smooth, glowing skin, dazzling blue eyes—the usual. "You don't seem like you're from around here," he observed, trying to engage her in conversation.

"Well, I came here to visit a friend of mine, or at least I thought we were friends."

"Friends? Well, it's not as simple as it sounds," he replied cryptically, offering her the necklace, which she accepted with a slow nod of gratitude. She admired the simple elegance of the necklace; it was a stark departure from the extravagant jewelry she was accustomed to.

"Why can't everything be free?" She muttered under her breath.

"Well, that would be communism. It sounds appealing, but it's not necessarily a practical idea for everything to be free," he explained.

"How much do I owe you?" she interjected, feeling a sense of obligation.

"How about I show you around the town? We can see some places here and there—nothing special, just a simple stroll," he suggested. The queen hesitated for a moment, weighing her options, before accepting his offer. After all, she had no money on her, and the prospect of exploring the town seemed far more appealing than facing Sera's wrath for sneaking out.

"I actually never got your name," he added. "You offered me a tour, not me giving you my name," she added. Suddenly he stopped on his tracks and smiled, "I don't know why but I feel there is something special about you that I can't get my teeth on."

The queen's curiosity was piqued as she regarded him with surprise. "Special? How so?" she inquired, her interest growing.

He shrugged nonchalantly. "I can't quite put my finger on it. It's just a feeling I get."

She tilted her head slightly, studying him intently. "Well, I suppose we'll have to see if your feeling holds any truth," she said with a hint of amusement in her voice.

With that, they resumed their stroll through the bustling streets, the young man guiding the way with ease as they explored the town together.

As they approached a seemingly abandoned building in the heart of the town, the young man's voice rang out with urgency. "Wait, don't go there!"

The queen's stubbornness prevailed as she moved towards the abandoned building, heedless of the young man's warning. Lost in her thoughts, she paid no heed to his caution until he grabbed her hand suddenly.

A heavy weight settled in his chest, as if gravity was increased around him, making it hard to breathe. With a gasp, he was forced to release her hand, his heart pounding in his ears. The queen snapped out of her reverie, her gaze shifting slowly to the young man before she spoke.

"Let's continue," she said quietly and unfazed.

"What's that place?" she asked, curiosity etched into her tone as they walked away.

"Well... I'm not entirely sure," he replied, still shaken from the strange sensation he'd felt earlier. "But everyone says it's bad news. Some folks claim it's a hotspot for cult activity, others swear they've seen monsters lurking around. But no one knows the whole story."

"Hmm..." the queen murmured, suddenly halting in her tracks and glancing back as if sensing something different.

"What's the matter?" he inquired, his concern evident.

"I think I need to leave," she stated abruptly, a sense of unease lingering in her demeanor.

"But we haven't finished exploring," he protested, but the queen remained resolute in her decision to depart.

"Well, can we meet again tomorrow?" he asked, hoping for a chance to continue their encounter. However, the queen seemed distracted, offering a nonchalant reply of "whatever" before vanishing into the crowd.

Left bewildered, he stood alone, pondering his encounter with such a strange young lady

She momentarily felt a shift in the atmosphere. The bustling sounds of the market seemed to fade into the background, replaced by a subtle, almost imperceptible tension. The hairs on the back of her neck stood on end, and a sense of unease settled over her. The normally vibrant town felt suddenly alien, its warmth replaced by an eerie chill that seemed to cling to her.

She came to a halt, her gaze sharpening as she scanned her surroundings. The market continued to buzz around her, oblivious to the shift in energy. Despite her outward calm, her senses were alert, picking up on an undercurrent of something sinister that had begun to seep into the bustling scene.

Deciding it was best to go somewhere away from everyone, walking a bit further, she halted and muttered without a hint of fear, "Who are you, and why were you following me?" Sinister laughter echoed from the surroundings, and suddenly, a mysterious figure materialized right in front of her. "Who are you?"

"Well, well, if it isn't the demon among men," it declared, but she sensed something was off with this new entity. "What do you want?" she demanded.

"I want to see how powerful you truly are, Queen Ivana," it replied, and Ivana knew it must have been spying on her to know her true identity with such confidence.

Without hesitation, it went on the offensive, leaving only dark smoke in its wake. Unfazed, the queen dodged its attacks, but it continued to assault her relentlessly, as if trying to end her life. "What are you after?" she demanded, slowly drawing away from him.

"Ivana, let's see your true nature," it declared, launching another attack. This time, it was faster and stronger, and the queen struggled to keep up in her current form. She couldn't allow herself to lose control again. "Stop denying your nature."

The queen couldn't continue as she was growing weaker, and she vowed never to use her powers again after her last battle. Just as the figure was about to land another blow, another figure appeared between them, blocking its punches. Surprisingly, it was the King of the East, though not surprising to her majesty.

"Are you alright?" he asked, concerned for the worn-out queen. "I'm fine," she replied.

"Alright, allow me to handle this," he said, stretching out his hands to summon a powerful sword adorned with magical gems and inscriptions, befitting a powerful king.

"Ah, King of the East, I only want her," the figure declared.

"If you want her, you'll have to get through me first," the king replied, as if trying to win the queen's favor. And so the battle continued, this time with the clash of the king's sword against the figure's dark powers. Strangely enough, the figure suddenly stopped and declared, "Today might not be my day," before disappearing, leaving behind a black residue.

"What exactly was that thing?" the king asked, perplexed. "Have you ever seen something like it?" The queen remained silent as she moved towards the residue, squatting to touch it.

"Stop! What if it's poisonous?" the king exclaimed.

Ivana ignored the king's warning and touched the residue cautiously. It felt cold and viscous to the touch, sending shivers down her spine. As she examined it, she noticed faint whispers emanating from the dark substance, whispering promises of power and darkness.

"This is a dark residue of high concentration." she murmured, her voice barely audible. "But I've never encountered anything like it before."

The king watched her with a mixture of concern and curiosity. "Should we dispose of it?" he asked, eyeing the residue warily.

The queen shook her head. "No, I need to study it further. It might hold clues about our enemy's intentions."

The king nodded in understanding. "Very well. But let's return to the palace. You need to rest and recover from this encounter."

"I don't need you to pretend as if you care, I never knew you could be so disgusting," she declared, "you want me to marry just because of an alliance."

The king sighed, frustration evident in his expression. "Ivana, please reconsider. We've been allies for so long. Don't let one disagreement destroy everything we've built together."

But the queen remained resolute, her gaze unwavering. "I cannot ignore what happened. Our paths diverge now, and I must follow mine alone. I don't need anyone."

"But.." he was suddenly stopped by the cold dark look in her eyes.

With a heavy heart, the king nodded. "Very well. But know that my door is always open to you, should you ever choose to return."

The tension between them lingered, a silent reminder of the rift that had formed between their kingdoms. As they parted ways, the queen couldn't help but wonder what the future held for both of them, and whether they would ever be able to reconcile their differences.

As she made her way back to the palace, the queen couldn't shake off the feeling of unease that lingered from her encounter with the mysterious figure. She knew that more challenges lay ahead, and she needed to be prepared to face them, whatever they may be.

Chapter 7

Ivana returned to the palace, still eager to retreat to the comfort of her clan. Lately, the tensions of this place had been wearing on her nerves. But that wasn't her immediate concern, right now. If Sera discovered she had sneaked out without informing her, she'd be in big trouble.

As she hurriedly slipped into her room, mindful of the late hour, she closed the door behind her and leaned against it, sighing in relief.

"Welcome, your majesty," a voice spoke from the darkness.

"Ah!" Ivana exclaimed in shock as Sera emerged from the darkness, igniting a lantern that illuminated the room and revealed her familiar face.

Queen Ivana held Sera in high regard, seeing her as both a motherly figure and a friend, even surpassing her own late mother. However, she despised seeing Sera angry with her. In the past, Sera would discipline her if she misbehaved as a child, but since Ivana's coronation as the queen of the demon clan, their roles had somewhat reversed, though not entirely. But the only person that is allowed to shout or punish her is only Sera, and Sera alone.

"Oh, it's you," Ivana replied calmly as she made her way to the bed.

"Where did you go?" concern etched on her face. "Why didn't you ask me to accompany you?"

"Sera, you're always worrying. Why can't you relax and enjoy life?" Ivana added with a smirk.

"I suppose you find it amusing, but you don't understand how many people look up to you, our clan, and especially me. Yet, you act as though your decisions won't impact any of us," Sera emphasized.

"Sera, do you think I wanted to be the queen of the demon clan? All I desired was freedom, but all of you constantly remind me of my duties, of the expectations placed upon me. Sometimes, I wish I were dead," Ivana replied, her voice tinged with resignation. "That's all I ever wished for, to just die."

Sera's expression softened as she listened to Ivana's words, sometimes forgetting, the queen never did have an easy life at the beginning . She moved closer to her, placing a comforting hand on her shoulder.

"Ivana, I understand it's not easy for you. But you have a responsibility to our clan, to our people. They rely on you, they believe in you," Sera said gently.

Ivana sighed, feeling the weight of her responsibilities pressing down on her. "I know, Sera. But sometimes, it feels like I'm suffocating under the weight of it all."

"I know it's overwhelming, but you're not alone. I'm here for you, always," Sera reassured her, her voice filled with sincerity.

Ivana managed a faint smile, grateful for Sera's unwavering support. "Thank you, Sera. I don't know what I'd do without you."

"Yeah, yeah, stubborn girl, where did you go off to?" Sera questioned, still not completely trusting her.

"I just went for a stroll, to see the scenery, you know, normal people stuff," Ivana replied, meeting an eyebrow raised. "Oh, they said that he had left before I reached there, to a place that nobody knew."

"Why do I get the feeling like I still don't trust you?" Sera said, her suspicion evident.

"Why would I lie to a sweet friend like you?" Ivana added with a smile, she knew her smile could never deceive Sera.

"Alright! No problem, you will eventually spill the complete truth," Sera emphasized.

Ivana lie comfortably on Sera's lap, a soft smile playing on her lips. She looked up at Sera with a glint of mischief in her eyes. "I am a good girl," she said with a playful tone, her words a gentle reminder of her sometimes childlike demeanor.

Sera chuckled softly, her hand brushing through Ivana's hair in a soothing gesture. The room was dimly lit, the soft glow of the lantern casting dancing shadows on the walls. The warm, flickering light created a tranquil atmosphere, contrasting sharply with the queen's usually stern and imposing presence.

For a while, they sat in serene silence. The gentle rise and fall of Ivana's breathing was the only sound that punctuated the quiet, each exhale a testament to the calm that had settled over her. The tension that had accompanied her earlier had dissipated, leaving behind a peaceful stillness.

As time passed, Ivana's breathing grew deeper and more rhythmic. The soft, contented sighs she made as she drifted into sleep were almost imperceptible. Sera watched with a mix of affection and amusement, marveling at how quickly Ivana had yield to slumber.

"Wow," Sera murmured softly, her voice barely above a whisper. She looked down at the queen, a bemused smile on her face. "I seriously wonder how she does it." The ease with which Ivana fell asleep seemed almost magical, a stark contrast to the queen's usual guarded demeanor. Perhaps, Sera thought, Ivana was simply exhausted from the day's events or perhaps it was just a part of her unique nature. Either way, the sight of Ivana sleeping so peacefully was a rare and precious moment that Sera cherished.

Sera continued to sit quietly, her thoughts drifting as she kept a watchful eye on the queen. The calm of the room was a welcome respite, and she allowed herself to enjoy the tranquility of the moment, knowing that it was fleeting but deeply cherished, until she noticed something strange.

"Sera, what are you doing?" Ivana's voice startled her as she quickly brushed off the particles.

"Nothing, just... cleaning," Sera stammered, trying to hide her concern.

Ivana raised an eyebrow, her gaze piercing. "You're acting strange. What's wrong?"

Sera hesitated for a moment, then decided to speak up. "I found these strange particles on your clothes. Where did they come from?"

Ivana's expression remained neutral, but there was a hint of tension in her voice as she replied, "It's nothing. Probably just dust from the room."

But Sera wasn't convinced. There was something off about those particles, something unsettling. She made a mental note to keep an eye on Ivana, she needed to uncover what she was hiding.

Ivana woke up early but remained in bed, unable to shake off the memory of the strange encounter from yesterday. Since the issue with the Kingdom of the East arose, things had only grown increasingly bizarre.

The queen lay curled up on her bed, her skin covered in goosebumps as she pondered the mysterious things surrounding the East Kingdom. Sensing something amiss, she couldn't shake off the feeling of unease.

After a while, she decided to take a stroll around the palace yard, hoping to distract herself with the beauty of the flowers and gardens. However, her serenity was shattered when she came face to face with the same young man she had encountered at the market. She froze, fearing he might recognize her despite her attempts to conceal her identity. But it was avoidable as he began to approach her.

"Wow, I never thought I might see you again, especially here," he marveled as he greeted her.

"I could say the same," she added.

"I work here," he replied as he continued. "What about you, do you also work here cause I have never seen you around? "

"I am not from around here, we just came for a visit," she added to be met with a questioning look from his face. "we?" She needed to come up with a lie that could fool him, without risking him knowing her true identity.

"I work for the demon queen."

The young man's eyes widened with surprise, his expression a mixture of disbelief and fascination. "The queen of the demon clan?" he echoed, his voice tinged with disbelief.

The queen nodded casually, enjoying the intrigue she was weaving. "Yes, she took me in as her personal attendant," she garnished, weaving a web of deception with ease.

His fascination seemed to grow, and he leaned in a bit closer, his curiosity piqued. "What's it like working for her? Is she as fearsome as they say?"

The queen chuckled inwardly, masking her true thoughts behind a composed facade. "Oh, she's not so bad once you get to know her," she replied cryptically, reveling in the game of secrets and half-truths.

"Isn't it scary with her witchcraft thing?"

The young man's question about the queen possessing witchcraft ability struck a nerve with Ivana. She was accustomed to the rumors and superstitions surrounding her clan and her especially, but it still irked her to hear it spoken aloud.

"Witchcraft?" she repeated, her tone incredulous. "I wouldn't call it that. It's more like… unique abilities."

She paused, sensing the need to clarify. "You see, the demon clan has long been misunderstood. Our abilities are not rooted in witchcraft or darkness. They are simply a part of who we are, just like any other talent or skill. It wasn't something she chose to acquire, it was forced on her...."

Before she could elaborate further, Sera's voice echoed through the garden, calling for the queen's attention. Ivana felt a surge of relief at the interruption, grateful for the chance to avoid delving into a conversation she'd rather avoid.

"Sorry, duty calls," she apologized to the young man, offering a polite smile. "Perhaps we can discuss this further another time."

With that, Ivana quickly made her way to where Sera was waiting, leaving the young man to ponder her words on his own.

As Ivana approached Sera, she could sense her curiosity brewing like a storm on the horizon.

"Who was that?" Sera inquired, her eyes scanning the garden for any lingering presence.

"Just someone I met briefly," Ivana replied casually, hoping to brush off any further probing.

Sera raised an eyebrow skeptically. "Seemed like quite the conversation from where I was standing. Knowing you, I know you don't like idle conversation."

Ivana sighed inwardly, knowing that Sera wouldn't let this go easily. "It was nothing, just idle chatter. Now, what did you need?"

Sera hesitated, her expression shifting as if she were debating whether to press further. Finally, she relented. "Just wanted to remind you about the meeting with the council later today."

Ivana nodded, grateful for the change of subject. "Right, I'll be there."

With that settled, Sera gave a nod of satisfaction before heading back into the palace. Ivana watched her go, feeling a mixture of relief and apprehension. She knew she couldn't keep her encounter with the young man a secret forever, but for now, she was content to let it remain in the shadows.

She went to meet the man, and their conversation continued. The man asked, "That looks like the queen's mistress too, Sera, I think." Ivana was surprised that he even knew her name but couldn't recognize her. A simple man, she smiled. "Oh yes, she is my senior mistress."

"Even with that talk, what are you actually doing here?" she asked, surprised to see him in the palace. The man explained that he was actually working under Maxym, who was the king's economic expert. Ivana was astonished to meet someone like him, which made her goal of coming to the kingdom worthwhile.

"Wait, are you also an expert?" she asked. "Yes, but I haven't been certified. My old man refuses to allow me to stretch my wings," he said, pausing to think before continuing, "but I have great ideas that could help, even if he thinks they're foolish."

Her maids were getting too close as everyone was looking for her, and she didn't want the young man to be ensnared in the demands of her royal status. So, she pulled him aside, and they slipped out of the palace for a stroll.

As they walked away from the palace, Ivana felt a sense of freedom she hadn't experienced in a long time. The young man, whose name she had later found to be Alex, the Alex that Sera had been disturbing her about, seemed genuinely interested in his ideas and perspective, without the weight of her royal title clouding their interaction.

"So, what are these great ideas of yours?" she asked, genuinely intrigued by his passion.

Alex's eyes lit up as he began to explain his innovative concepts for improving the kingdom's economy, his enthusiasm infectious. Ivana found herself drawn into his vision, impressed by his creativity and determination.

As they continued their conversation, Ivana couldn't help but wonder what it would be like to have someone like Alex in her clan, someone with vision and just passion, but who knows how he would feel if he found out that she was the queen.

As they walked further, she asked, "I heard the queen was looking for an economic expert like you. Do you think you could work for her?" Alex was taken aback for a moment, but he replied, "It would be a nice experience, but I don't think my family would agree. Working for the demon clan or your queen could get me into trouble—no offense."

Ivana's expression changed. She wasn't surprised to hear this from him. Everyone seemed to fear the clan for one reason or another. But regardless of what this man said, she didn't care. One way or another, he would be working for the demon clan by next week.

"So you do fear the clan," she replied.

"Ah, no, not at all. It's actually your queen. Her character is strange. I've heard that she behaves heartlessly. Some say she isn't even human," he explained casually, tossing a small stone across the road. The stone skipped along the cobblestones, disrupting the otherwise serene atmosphere.

The casualness of his tone seemed to underline the gravity of his words, and a thoughtful silence hung between them as they both absorbed the implication. The day had been a whirlwind, and his casual dismissal of the queen's peculiar nature felt oddly out of place amidst the tension.

"Hmmm... well..." She began, her brow furrowed as she tried to formulate a response, but before she could articulate her thoughts, the sudden clanking of armor interrupted her.

In a swift and startling move, the royal guards appeared around them, their swords drawn and gleaming menacingly in the sunlight. The guards formed a tight circle, their presence imposing and unyielding.

"What is the meaning of this?" he demanded, his voice rising in a mixture of surprise and indignation. The guards, their expressions set in stern resolve, did not waver as they awaited an explanation. The abrupt shift from casual conversation to this tense standoff heightened the sense of urgency and unease.

"Sorry, but the queen was caught trying to kill his majesty," they explained. Alex was confused. "Which queen? There is no queen around here," he replied, still not aware of her true identity. Meanwhile, Ivana was shocked to hear that someone impersonated her to attack the king but still failed — so shameful. But she hadn't been in the palace throughout the day.

The men pressed on relentlessly, their attempts to capture her growing more aggressive. Despite their efforts, she could sense an underlying darkness in their motives, a malicious intent that made her wary. The air around them seemed to thicken with tension, heightening her unease.

"Stop, that," Alex called out, his voice carrying a note of urgency as he tried to intervene. His warning was meant to halt the men, but they continued their advance, their resolve unshaken.

The situation escalated rapidly. Without warning, the men suddenly collapsed, their bodies falling lifelessly to the ground in a swift and shocking display. Alex's eyes widened in disbelief as he watched the scene unfold. The once intimidating group now lay motionless before him, their dark intentions abruptly and violently cut short.

Alex turned around, his gaze drawn to Ivana. His shock deepened as he saw her eyes, once warm and familiar, now completely black. Dark veins pulsed and twisted around her neck, a sinister and otherworldly glow emanating from them. The transformation was startling, an unsettling shift from the person he had known.

Overwhelmed by a mix of fear and surprise, Alex stumbled backward. His heart raced in his chest, each beat a stark reminder of the terror that now gripped him. The once familiar young lady had become a vision of horror, her presence now a formidable and fearsome figure. As he fell to the ground, his mind reeled with the unsettling realization of the change that had overtaken her.

"Wait, you're the queen?" he exclaimed in disbelief. Ivana looked at him with a knowing gaze, realizing that the friendship they had almost formed had been shattered by her true nature - that of a demon.

Ivana remained silent, her gaze piercing through Alex as if searching for something within him. She could see the fear and confusion etched on his face, but at this point there is no point in trying to win him over.

Finally, she spoke in a voice that seemed to resonate with an otherworldly power, "Yes, I am the queen of the demon clan."

Alex's eyes widened in both awe and terror at her admission. He struggled to comprehend the reality of the situation, his mind racing with questions and doubts.

"But... why?" he managed to stammer out, his voice trembling with uncertainty.

Ivana's expression softened slightly, a flicker of regret crossing her features. "It's complicated," she replied cryptically.

Before Alex could utter another word, the sound of approaching footsteps caught Ivana's attention. The rhythmic thud of boots grew louder, and she turned her gaze toward the source of the noise.

"Well, Alex," she said with a casual shrug, her tone devoid of the warmth it once held. "Whether you're afraid of the demon clan or not, I'm taking you there." Her face had lost the enchanting smile she had previously worn, replaced by an expression of cold determination. It was as though a different persona had taken her place, one far removed from the charming young lady Alex had known.

Just then, the king and his men arrived, their presence commanding immediate respect. Accompanied by Ivana's advisor, Sera, and her entourage, they surrounded the area with an air of authority and menace. The king's voice cut through the tension as he issued a grim warning, threatening death if any attempt was made to escape.

Ivana's reaction was swift. In a fluid motion, she pulled Alex into her embrace, her grip firm and unyielding, as he held tightly to his neck. Her voice was cold and resolute as she issued a stern warning to the king's men. "Touch them and he dies," she threatened, her eyes flashing with a fierce intensity.

The king's response was immediate and chilling. "Dispose of him; he means nothing to me," he said dismissively. His words were laced with a ruthless indifference that left Alex stunned. The king's callousness was a stark contrast to the gravity of the situation, and it sent a shiver down Alex's spine.

The queen smiled slowly, easing the pressure of Alex's neck as she replied, "And they call me heartless. But actually, Your Majesty," she said, raising her hand as if about to snap her fingers before continuing, "I didn't attempt to harm you if that's why you're afraid of me. And if I did you would have been dead by now."

"Then surrender and let's discuss it in the palace," the king proposed, his tone steady and authoritative.

Ivana's response was a chilling laugh, one that carried a devilish edge. "You and me? Ha! There's something suspicious about you, and you'd better hope I don't uncover it. But in any case, I've achieved what I wanted," she said, her gaze shifting to Alex with a predatory gleam in her eyes.

The king sneered, his voice dripping with derision. "Him? What are you going to do with someone like him? A trash?"

Ivana's lips curled into a cold, mocking smile. "Recycle him," she replied, her tone laced with a dark humor that sent a shiver down Alex's spine.

The king's patience snapped. "Who cares? You're not leaving. Guards, seize them!" he ordered, his voice echoing with authority.

Ivana's eyes narrowed dangerously, a flash of malevolence in their depths. "Ha! You think you can make me stay?" she retorted, her voice a low, menacing growl.

Without warning, she snapped her fingers with a decisive crack. In an instant, a tangible sense of displacement gripped the scene. The air seemed to ripple and warp around them, a disturbing distortion that made the world feel unreal.

A shiver-inducing cold enveloped the space as if the very fabric of reality was being torn apart. The king's eyes widened in shock and disbelief as he watched in stunned silence. The faces of his guards reflected panic, their usual composure shattered by the queen's display of power.

Suddenly, with an unpleasant lurch, Sera, Ivana, her maids, her entourage, and Alex vanished. The scene was left eerily empty, the only sound the faint echo of Ivana's laughter lingering in the air. The king stood there, his mouth wide open, grappling with the sudden and unsettling realization of the queen's formidable power. The once bustling space was now a cold, silent void, leaving His Majesty to ponder the sheer might of the queen of the demon clan.

Chapter 8

Everything went pitch black. Time seemed to stop as reality felt frozen, yet somehow still moving. The voices of the queen and the king echoed faintly, their words drifting away into the void. The darkness stretched and warped, then suddenly erupted into flashes of light and noise.

Sparks and streaks of lightning ran through the void, growing more intense with each passing moment. The air crackled and buzzed as if the very fabric of space was about to tear apart. The noise built to a deafening roar, creating a sense of chaotic energy all around and it all seemed to be coming from one person, that wasn't even there.

With a thunderous bang, a burst of dark smoke surrounded them. In an instant, they reappeared in the palace courtyard, right in front of the queen's grand residence. The familiar sight of the demon clan's palace felt both comforting and surreal, as if they had never left, despite the undeniable sense of teleportation.

"We're back?" a maid exclaimed, her voice trembling with relief as she took in their familiar surroundings.

Alex stood there, his heart racing with adrenaline. The teleportation had felt like a scene from a nightmare, but here he was, facing the queen herself. Her eyes were completely black, and dark veins pulsed visibly around her neck, beating with the energy she had just used. Smoke still curled from her back. It was very clear that she was exhausted.

He couldn't look away from Ivana. Despite the chaotic teleportation and the extraordinary display of her abilities, she remained calm and composed. To her, it seemed like just another ordinary day, her demeanor unmoved by the wonderful display of her power.

The queen caught his lingering stare, and for a moment, their eyes locked in a silent exchange. Alex quickly averted his gaze, feeling a shiver run down his spine at the intensity of her presence. It was always strange how the queen's appearance made her seem approachable and likable, but once you made contact with her eyes, it was like staring into pure darkness.

"Are you okay?" she asked, moving closer to him. He stepped back instinctively, a shiver running down his spine. The intense dark energy emanating from her was almost palpable.

"I... I am fine," he stammered, his fear evident in his voice.

"Relax," she said calmly, moving closer. "If I had wanted to harm you, I would have done that back at the East Kingdom." Her expression was clear and composed, but her presence was still unsettling.

"Your Majesty, your nose," a maid said urgently, her voice filled with concern. As she touched it, her hands came away stained with blood.

"Ah! The consequences," Ivana gasped before collapsing. Alex reacted quickly, catching her before she hit the ground.

"Your Majesty!" he called out, but Ivana remained unresponsive.

"Relax! She's just burnt out," Sera said firmly, taking charge. She gently pulled Ivana away from Alex's grasp. "She hasn't teleported this many people before."

Alex's eyes widened in realization. He understood now that teleporting such a large group had taken a toll on Ivana. She had done it to protect everyone, despite the strain it placed on her.

"Hey, you," Sera directed one of the maidens, "take this young man to one of the guest rooms." She gestured towards Alex, who was still reeling from the teleportation, his senses not fully recovered. He could barely make out the voices around him as he was led away.

As Ivana slowly regained consciousness, she found herself nestled on a plush bed, the softness a stark contrast to the harshness of her recent ordeal. Sera hovered over her, worry etched deeply on her face, the lines of concern unmistakable.

"You're awake, Your Majesty," Sera said, her voice trembling with relief.

Ivana blinked, struggling to clear the fog from her mind. The images of the strange figure and the sudden teleportation whirled around in her thoughts, leaving her feeling disoriented and drained.

"Sera, what happened?" Ivana asked, her voice still groggy from sleep.

"You collapsed," Sera explained, her concern evident. "It seems you overexerted yourself. But don't worry, you're safe now."

Ivana nodded slowly, but her mind was already racing with questions. How had she managed to teleport so many people at once? And who was that mysterious figure that had attacked her in the town?

"Sera," Ivana began, her voice tinged with uncertainty. "Did you see Alex with me?"

Sera paused, her brow furrowing. "Alex? Yes, he was right there with you when we arrived back at the courtyard. You remember him, right?"

Ivana's heart skipped a beat. Alex had been there? But that didn't make sense—she had no memory of him being by her side during the teleportation.

"No, Sera," Ivana replied firmly, shaking her head. "I don't remember seeing Alex. Are you sure he was there?"

Sera's expression shifted from concern to confusion. "But Your Majesty, he was right there. I saw him myself. He even caught you when you fell unconscious."

Ivana's thoughts raced with possibilities. Could it be that she had somehow missed seeing Alex? Or was there something more sinister at play? For some moment she sat quietly thinking of what could have happened, could it be the teleportation?

She hissed in realization. The side effects of mass teleportation were significant—if not handled carefully, it could mix and even harm or kill those within the teleportation void. The immense strain on the mind during such a process often led to gaps in memory. It was why most people couldn't recall the sensation of teleportation. Despite the seeming immediacy, the process took a considerable amount of time and required an enormous amount of energy to breach the fabric of space. But still it would feel like it occurred in an instant.

"Never mind."

"Good morning, your majesty," Sera greeted. Meanwhile, Ivana was sitting at the edge of her bed, inspecting the dark scar left by the excess power she used when she teleported everyone yesterday. It was getting more serious than the other times, she still couldn't make out why it always formed when she was using her power, even just a bit of it.

"What's good about the morning," Ivana replied coldly.

"Wow, someone's in a bad mood today," Sera smiled, but the queen ignored her—as usual.

Ivana was still thinking about why her memory was foggy from yesterday. She couldn't remember some details, especially those involving Alex. Some of the memories usually come back on their own.

"Your majesty, are you still worried about yesterday?" Sera asked, but the queen, lost in thought, ignored her yet again.

Sera quietly approached her and placed her hands on the queen's shoulder, bringing her back to reality. "You are not in this alone. You have us, all of us here in the clan," Sera emphasized.

Ivana slowly patted Sera's hand and offered a gentle smile. "Of course, I know that," she said warmly, but still felt forced.

"Then turn that frown upside down," Sera said suddenly, her tone shifting to a playful command. "Now, get off the bed."

Ivana looked at Sera in surprise. "Wow! My own bed and you're kicking me out?"

"Well, if you don't get up, you might find yourself washing those sheets later," Sera teased, a mischievous smile playing on her lips.

"You can't make me do that. I'm the queen of this clan. With a snap of my fingers, I can have every sheet in the clan cleaned," Ivana boasted, only to fall silent when she saw the look on Sera's face. It was a look that clearly said, Are you sure about that?

"Alright, alright! I'm getting up," Ivana conceded, rolling her eyes as she pushed herself off the bed. She stepped away as Sera began to pull off the dirty sheets. With a sigh, Ivana made her way toward the balcony, where she could enjoy some fresh air and clear her thoughts.

The balcony faced the royal garden, offering a breathtaking view of the lush, vibrant expanse that stretched out below. From here, one could see the dense, mysterious forest of the demon clan, its towering trees forming a dark, almost impenetrable barrier at the garden's edge. The garden itself was a masterpiece, designed to reflect the rich vegetative diversity of the clan. It boasted both common and rare flowers, their colors blending harmoniously in a display of natural beauty. At the garden's center stood a grand fountain, its water sparkling in the sunlight, visible in its entirety from Ivana's vantage point.

Yet, despite its beauty, Ivana had never taken a liking to the garden. It wasn't the flowers or the fountain that bothered her, but rather the memory of the person who had designed it. The sight of the garden always stirred something uncomfortable within her.

"Don't forget you have a court meeting later," Sera reminded her from behind.

"Okay," Ivana replied absentmindedly, her attention suddenly captured by a small movement below. Her eyes focused on a gray cat prowling through the garden. It was an unfamiliar sight—Ivana had never seen such a cat in the palace before. Maybe it's new, she mused. With hundreds of people working for her, it could easily belong to anyone, yet the sight of it intrigued her. The cat moved with a quiet confidence, as if it owned the place.

Ivana called out, "Sera! Do we have a gray cat?"

"Your Majesty, with all the pets and animals in the palace, how would I know if we have a gray cat?" Sera replied.

Ivana's eyes remained fixed on the cat as it suddenly stopped moving and turned to stare right at her. There was something unsettling about the way it held her gaze. Then, its gray fur began to darken. Ivana leaned in, watching as the cat started twitching and curling up into a tight ball. Dark particles began to swirl around its body, and before she could fully comprehend what was happening, the cat burst into a cloud of dark particles, reforming into a human shape.

Ivana's heart raced. She knew instantly—it was that strange being that had attacked her in the East Kingdom. There was no time to think. She leaped off the balcony, a nearly three-story drop

"What? Your Majesty!" Sera shouted in alarm as she saw Ivana jump.

Ivana landed with ease, the ground denting slightly under the force of her landing. Without a moment's hesitation, she sprinted after the figure, determined not to let it escape again.

The entity sprinted through the palace garden, with Ivana chasing after it, determination blazing in her eyes. They raced past manicured hedges and vibrant flowers, the once-peaceful garden now a backdrop to their intense pursuit. Suddenly, the entity came to an abrupt halt.

Ivana didn't hesitate. She lunged at it with all her strength, her punch fueled by the raw power of her resolve. This was no time to hold back—this creature had stalked her in the East, and now it was here, in her home. But the entity blocked her strike effortlessly. The ground beneath them shattered, forming a crater from the impact of her attack.

"Queen Ivana the Third," the entity intoned, gripping her hand tightly, "I'm not here to fight you—at least, not yet."

Ivana struggled to free herself, glaring at the strange, almost formless being. "Who or what are you?" she demanded.

The entity ignored her question. "You have one month. Two choices: accept the terms of the King of the East, or lose your kingdom—and your life."

"Isn't that the same thing?" she scoffed, her expression shifting as a realization hit her. "Wait, did the King of the East send you?"

"He lacks the power to do so," the entity replied, its voice hinting at darker forces at play.

"Then who?" Ivana pressed.

"You'll find out if you agree to the terms," it said, its tone firm.

Ivana smirked. "Too bad for you, I'm stubborn. And whatever you just said? I've already forgotten."

Almost instantly, Ivana aimed a powerful kick at the entity. But it blocked her effortlessly and countered with a swift kick to her stomach. The force of the blow sent her reeling, and she collapsed to her knees, gasping in pain.

"Don't think that just because you possess the power of the Nether, you can do as you please," he said, his voice icy and menacing.

Ivana, struggling to catch her breath, managed to ask, "Wait, power of the Nether? What's that?"

The entity leaned in, his face inches from hers. "Ivana, thirty days," he whispered ominously.

Before she could react, he vanished in a swirl of dark smoke. Ivana seethed with frustration. She had never been struck by anyone and they survived to tell the tale. This entity was different. How was the King of the East connected to this formidable being? And what did the power of the Nether mean?

The questions burned in her mind as she fought to regain her composure. The intensity of the encounter left her shaken, but she knew it wasn't the worst she'd faced.

"Your Majesty! Your Majesty!" Sera shouted, running up with a group of armed guards. Panting heavily, she demanded, "What on earth were you thinking, jumping off the balcony and running like that?"

Sera's eyes widened as she noticed the same black particles she had seen before. "Where did you get these?"

Ivana hesitated, realizing that explaining would only complicate matters. It was better if they remained unaware of the powerful entity. They looked up to her for answers, and the idea of something more powerful than her could shatter the sense of security they relied on.

"Well, what?" Sera interjected, her eyes filled with concern.

"It's nothing," Ivana replied with a forced smile.

"Nothing? You think this is funny? Seriously, Queen Ivana, sometimes I don't understand what's going on in that head of yours. It's like you're hiding something from us," Sera exclaimed, frustration creeping into her voice.

Ivana knew she had to think quickly to ease Sera's suspicions. "I was just trying to practice my agility," she lied smoothly. "I thought it would help me stay sharp. And the black particles? They're from my scars—they shed a lot."

Sera raised an eyebrow, clearly not buying the explanation. "Practicing agility by jumping off balconies? Your Majesty, please be more careful. We worry about you."

Ivana nodded, trying to appear genuinely sorry. "I will, Sera. I'm sorry for making you worry. I'll be more cautious in the future." Though, truth be told, "cautious" wasn't exactly in the queen's vocabulary—she was more inclined to leap from one crisis to the next, from one little thing to destroying half a kingdom.

Sera sighed, still skeptical but choosing to let it go for now. "Alright. Just remember, we're here for you. You don't have to handle everything on your own."

"Thank you, Sera," Ivana said, her smile more sincere this time. "I appreciate your concern."

But as she turned away, her mind raced with thoughts of the mysterious figure and the threat looming over her kingdom. She had thirty days to uncover the truth and protect her people from whatever danger was coming.

"Sera, I want Alex at the meeting."

Meanwhile, Alex was in the guest room, unable to sleep. The events of the past day replayed in his mind, sending shivers down his spine. He had spent time with the queen of the demon clan, thinking she was just an ordinary woman. Then he discovered that his own king wanted him dead. Despite being the assistant to the royal expert, he now questioned his worth. Trapped in the demon clan, he couldn't shake the feeling that the queen had ulterior motives for keeping him around.

"Just my luck," he muttered, feeling the weight of his situation.

A knock at the door snapped him out of his thoughts. His heart raced—it could be the queen. He hesitated, then opened the door, feeling relieved to see Sera standing there instead.

"Good morning, the queen's special guest," she greeted him with a cheerful smile.

"Special? What's so special about me?" he wondered silently.

"Good morning," he replied, trying to match her tone.

"Her Majesty has requested your presence at the morning meeting," Sera said, her words adding to his anxiety.

Before she could leave, Alex blurted out, "What's the queen like around here?"

Sera paused, then her expression turned mock-serious. "She's a monster. Everyone's terrified of her, even me—her personal assistant. And when she goes berserk, well... let's just say you don't want to be around."

Alex's face paled, and Sera couldn't hold back her laughter. "Relax, Alex, I'm just messing with you. She's actually nice, but she has her quirks. Just avoid giving her two answers to a single question. She really doesn't like contradictions."

"Contradictions?" he echoed, trying to keep up.

"Yeah, she likes people to be sure of what they say. If it's not an option, don't act confused. Just be confident."

Alex managed a small smile. "That's... interesting."

Sera noticed his lingering tension and gave him a reassuring pat on the shoulder. "Hey, don't overthink it. The queen's tough, but she's fair. Just be yourself, and you'll be fine. Besides, you've got me to keep you out of trouble."

Her playful tone eased some of his nerves, and Alex couldn't help but chuckle. "Thanks. I guess I needed that."

"That's the spirit!" she beamed. "Now, let's get going before we're late. And don't worry—I'll be there to back you up if the queen starts throwing any curveballs."

As they walked toward the meeting, Alex felt a little lighter. The thought of being in the same room with the queen was still daunting, but at least he knew he had at least someone like Sera around.

Chapter 9

Arriving at the courtroom, Alex found it already filled with elders, both young and old, along with various officials whose roles he couldn't discern. The room was more organized than anything he'd seen in the East, and its size was impressive. The wooden interior was magnificent, with intricately designed furniture adorned with gold lining. The high ceiling and massive marble pillars added to the grandeur. The entire courtroom was themed around fine dark wood, a material rare and expensive outside the demon clan. However, what truly captured Alex's attention was the magnificent throne at the far end of the room. It glittered with gold accents, its intricate design and elevated position exuding authority.

A servant guided Alex to his seat on the right side of the courtroom, opposite the elders. The queen had not yet arrived, but he could feel everyone's eyes on him, accompanied by whispers and curious glances. The tension in the room mirrored his own anxiety.

"Her Majesty, Queen Ivana the Third," an announcement echoed through the room. Instantly, the courtroom fell silent as all eyes turned toward the queen. She walked gracefully to her throne, dressed in her signature black and white attire. Her hair was beautifully styled, with plaited sections, and her lips were painted a deep, dark shade.

"It has been quite long, Your Majesty. Here is a proper welcome from your return from the East," declared Thomas, the newly appointed first elder, who had taken the position after the previous first elder's head was gruesomely displayed in the courtyard.

Ivana acknowledged Thomas with a nod, her expression neutral as she took her seat on the throne. The atmosphere was thick with tension as everyone awaited her words. She scanned the room, tapping her finger lightly on the arm of her throne—a simple gesture, but one that heightened the tension.

"Thank you, Thomas," Ivana finally spoke, her voice calm yet commanding. "It is good to be back among my people." As the tension in the room eased slightly, Alex felt a momentary relief—until her gaze suddenly locked onto him, sending a shiver down his spine.

"Now," Ivana continued, "let us address the matters at hand."

Thomas stepped forward. "Your Majesty, we have several issues that require your attention. But first, we must discuss the recent events involving our guest." He gestured toward Alex, drawing more attention his way.

Ivana's eyes narrowed slightly as she focused on Alex. "Alex, stand and introduce yourself."

With his nerves on edge, Alex stood and tried to steady himself, doing his best to maintain composure despite his uncertainty. "My name is Alex. I was brought here by Queen Ivana after an encounter in the East Kingdom."

The elders murmured among themselves, their whispers filling the room

"Silence," commanded Adrian, the queen's adviser, and the room fell quiet at once. "Alex, you are here because the Queen has hired you to be the clan's economic analyst."

Alex hesitated, glancing around the room. "I don't know much," he began. "But..."

"But he has decided to work for us, right?" Queen Ivana interjected, her gaze locking with Alex's. The way her eyes were so calm and relaxed, it felt like there was no escape. He hadn't agreed to work for her, but with the queen's reputation, arguing seemed futile.

The room erupted in whispers again, but Ivana remained serene.

Thomas nodded. "We will build our economy because this is what fuels our defensive and offensive capabilities."

"Now," Ivana said, her voice commanding once more, "let us move on to other pressing matters. Much has happened while we were away...."

As the discussions continued, Alex couldn't shake the feeling that he was now a pawn in a much larger game. He desperately wished the queen could understand why he couldn't work with them, but doubted she cared.

Despite all the rumors, he found himself captivated by the queen. The way she handled court matters with such ease and authority commanded respect, even though she was likely in her early twenties—much younger than the elders around her.

After the meeting, Alex wandered through the palace, admiring its stunning aesthetics. Every corner seemed to feature something intricately carved from dark wood. Lost in thought, he unexpectedly encountered the queen and her entourage.

Seeing him, she gestured for everyone to leave them alone.

"Good morning, Your Majesty," Alex greeted, bowing his head slightly.

She watched him with a cold stare and didn't bother to return his greeting.

"Good morning," Sera, who was present, quickly replied. "I hope your stay here has been pleasant."

He nodded. "Well, actually, it's been better than I expected."

Sera, noticing the queen's lack of response, nudged her gently. "Hey, why did you hit me?" Ivana snapped, turning to Sera with an angered look.

"He greeted you, and you didn't even care to reply or acknowledge him," Sera chided.

"So, do I look like I give a damn?" Ivana replied coldly. Turning back to Alex, she continued, "And Alex, I want you to meet Adrian, my advisor. He will show you around our businesses and trade. I expect your plans for improving them by next week."

Alex hesitated, clearing his throat. "Well, Your Majesty, I never actually agreed to work as your economic analyst."

Ivana's expression didn't change. "Well, Alex, unfortunately for you, I don't care. You serve the demon clan now until I permit you to go."

"But you can't just make me work for you. I appreciate you saving my life, but I'm better off returning to the East," he stated, trying to remain composed. Her calm demeanor still remained unchanged.

The queen squatted down to pick up a twig from the ground, ignoring his protest. "Ivana! For God's sake, sometimes try to act like you care instead of giving this nonchalant vibe," Sera interjected, trying to diffuse the growing tension.

"You can go," the queen said as she stood up, still playing with the twig. Alex felt a wave of relief until she added, "when you are dead."

Alex was speechless, but she continued, "If you still feel like I can't make you work for me, then I guess your lonely mother and younger sisters will have to pay with their blood. I can't save you and let you go scot-free. Haven't you heard? Blood for blood."

"What? Are you threatening me?" he asked, fear evident in his voice.

The twig in the queen's hand began to smoke, turning black before bursting into dust—a silent reminder of her powers.

"So, Alex, you have two options: meet Adrian or go back to the East and greet your family for me, especially your sisters, Lisa and Mia, and your mother with her large farm. She is really a virtuous woman," she declared. Alex's eyes widened as she described his family with chilling accuracy. How did she know? He couldn't afford to defy her now. She wouldn't even know his sister's names, he hadn't mentioned that to anyone, he always tries to keep his family name a secret.

Seeing the concern etched on his face, Sera tried once more. "Your Majesty, if he doesn't want to stay, we shouldn't force him. He has his own life to live."

Ivana's voice was calm, almost casual. "Sure, Alex, so when am I getting your plans? Anyway, I expect them by next week."

"But—" Before he could finish, the ground beneath him suddenly dented and concaved, as if something invisible had landed there with tremendous force.

"Your Majesty!" Sera yelled. "You could have killed him."

"But he's still standing, isn't he? For now," Ivana replied as she turned away, walking off.

Sera watched as fear gripped Alex. It was nothing new, but if he didn't comply, the queen might actually follow through on her threat.

"Sorry about that," Sera apologized. "Alex, my only advice is to do what she says for now. I'll try to talk her into letting you go, but I can't promise anything."

"Thanks," he replied simply, though his mind was racing with the weight of the impossible situation he found himself in.

Alex spent the rest of the day grappling with his predicament. The queen's cold threat echoed in his mind, leaving him with no real choice but to comply. Later, he met Adrian, the queen's advisor—a tall, stern-looking man with sharp features and an air of authority.

"Welcome, Alex," Adrian said, extending a hand. "Her Majesty has high expectations for you."

"Thank you," Alex replied, shaking his hand. "I'll do my best."

Adrian nodded. "Good. Let's start with a tour of our trading facilities."

As they walked through the palace and the surrounding areas, Adrian explained the intricacies of the demon clan's economy. Despite his initial resistance, Alex found himself intrigued by the complexity and efficiency of their systems. He realized there was much he could learn here, and perhaps even contribute to.

That evening, back in his guest room, Alex lay on his bed, staring at the ceiling. The day had been overwhelming, and he couldn't shake the image of the queen's cold, unwavering eyes. Just then, a soft knock on the door interrupted his thoughts.

"Come in," he called.

The door opened, and Sera entered, her expression gentle but serious. "How are you holding up?"

"I'm... managing," Alex replied, sitting up. "It's a lot to take in."

Sera nodded, taking a seat across from him. "The queen can be... intense. But she's not heartless, despite how she might seem. She carries a lot on her shoulders."

"Why does she have to be so threatening?" Alex asked, frustration creeping into his voice.

"She believes it's necessary to maintain control," Sera explained. "The demon clan isn't like other kingdoms. Strength and power are respected above all else. Showing any sign of weakness could lead to chaos. Her mother, Ivana the Second, engraved this mindset deeply in her."

Alex's eyes widened slightly. He'd heard of Ivana the Second—a name that inspired both awe and fear. "I understand that, but threatening my family?" Alex shook his head. "That's crossing a line."

"I agree," Sera said softly. "But that's why I'm here—to help you navigate this and, hopefully, to soften her approach."

Alex sighed, feeling a mix of gratitude and hopelessness. "Thank you, Sera. I appreciate your support."

Sera smiled. "You're welcome. Just hang in there, and do what you can to prove your value. It might be the only way to gain her trust."

The next morning, Alex was up early, determined to make the best of his situation. He met with Adrian again, diving into the details of their trade operations. As the days passed, he found himself becoming more involved, with his analysis proving valuable to the clan.

Meanwhile, Ivana observed from a distance, her cold exterior never wavering. Yet deep down, she was curious about this young man from the East who dared to challenge her. She wondered if there was more to him than met the eye.

One evening, after a particularly long day of meetings and planning, Alex found himself alone in one of the palace gardens. The moonlight cast a serene glow over the landscape, and he took a moment to appreciate the beauty around him.

As he stood there, lost in thought, he heard footsteps approaching. He turned to see Ivana, her expression unreadable.

"Good evening, Your Majesty," he greeted, bowing his head slightly.

Ivana nodded, her gaze fixed on him. "You've been working hard."

"Yes, Your Majesty. I don't exactly want to die," Alex replied as he smiled a little.

She studied him for a moment, then said, "The improvements you suggested are already making a difference."

"Thank you," Alex said, surprised by the compliment.

"But I still mean what I said before—I won't hesitate to take your life, or that of your family, if it comes to that." Ivana took a step closer and tilted her head a bit, her eyes intense. "I do this because my clan needs you. But I? I don't need you. So remember, you're helping people, not me."

With that, she turned and walked away, leaving Alex to ponder her words empty without a thought of feeling, unsalted with any emotion. For the first time, he glimpsed the woman beneath the cold, regal exterior, even if it wasn't in the way he'd hoped. And he wondered if, perhaps, there was a chance for understanding between them after all.

Chapter 10

It had been about a week since Alex was thrown into the demon clan, or more accurately, abducted into it. It felt like falling into a pit, with the only way out being through the very person who had put him there. Accepting this new role was tough, despite the queen's decent pay—probably more than what Kyson offered. Still, the situation was far from ideal.

What made it somewhat easier were the friendly clansmen. Except for the queen, the rest were kind and helpful. Working with them had made him more determined, and his efforts were already the talk of the town. He let out a heavy sigh, wiping sweat from his brow, and looked at the distance they had covered to lay the final rail.

"Yes! Finally, it's complete!"

"Wow, I thought we'd never finish it," one of the young workers said, pointing at the contraption Alex had designed. The cart, its metallic lustrous body now gleaming in the sunlight, was set on sturdy rails and featured a series of wooden crates arranged neatly. It was designed to facilitate the easy movement of goods between two nearby towns. The cart's wheels were intricately carved and fitted with metal bands to ensure smooth rolling.

"Yeah, it was challenging, but with all of you strong-willed men around, nothing is impossible," Alex replied, his enthusiasm evident. The workers cheered, celebrating their latest success. No matter how mad or angry he felt being here, these enthusiastic young men always made him have second thoughts, it was quite an egoistic feeling to have someone look up to you.

As word spread, a crowd began to gather, drawn by the news of the completed project and the rumor that the queen herself would be visiting, it was quite a big deal to see the queen, hardly leaving her palace, she would always send either Adrian or Sera in her place, the only time you will catch a glimpse of her was during the Clan's meeting or during battle's were she uses her abilities.

"Her majesty, Queen Ivana the Third," Adrian announced. The bustling crowd fell silent, everyone composing themselves in the presence of the queen. What was on everyone's mind was how the queen looked and gave off the same energy as her mother, but yet she wasn't completely like her. Something that everyone is grateful for.

Ivana walked calmly and majestically, her expression unreadable. Her eyes were fixed on Alex, who couldn't help but feel a bit nervous under her gaze. He quickly switched his gaze to Adrian, who was walking a bit close to the queen, the look on her face was unreadable. It was hollow without any grain of emotion, but it somehow felt like she was forced to be here, today.

"Wow, Alex, you have truly outdone yourself," Adrian commented as he viewed the contraption, marveling at how he was able to achieve this.

"What do you think, Your Majesty?" Adrian asked. She remained silent, her gaze firmly placed on Alex.

"Your Majesty, won't you comment on it?" Sera interjected, nudging her to at least say something encouraging.

"Great job." Her words came out simply, It was clear to everyone that she didn't mean it. Alex, feeling a surge of frustration, turned away and sighed. Despite his hard work, even against his will, she couldn't muster a genuine thank you or any appreciation for him or his crew.

He got angry and walked away, it was clear he was discouraged by her actions.

Sera pulled Ivana aside and whispered fiercely, "You need to acknowledge their effort. They've worked hard on this."

Ivana just stared into Sera without a muttering sound, she slowly picked up some gravel from the ground, still ignoring Sera.

"Ivana! For God's sake, even if you don't have any room for caring, have you considered the feelings of those around you?" Sera retorted, her voice edged with frustration. Ivana remained silent, throwing stones at a tree.

"What is wrong with you?" Sera yelled, finally grabbing the stones from Ivana's hand.

"Hey, don't shout at me," Ivana snapped. "I might allow you to be friendly around me, but you should know your place. Don't cross the line and stop acting as if you are my mother."

Sera fell silent, stunned by Ivana's harsh words. She just couldn't understand why Ivana was acting so differently today. Well, she always acts differently but today is special.

"Didn't you say you wanted to make the Demon Clan great and respected among the kingdoms? Didn't you promise everyone here that you would protect them?" Sera continued, her voice softer but still firm. She slowly returned the stones to Ivana's hand. "We might not have powers like you, but we have feelings. And I guess it would be better to be ruled by someone who cares than someone who just pretends to. Your nonchalant attitude might become the downfall of the clan, no matter your abilities."

"If you know what's best, go and apologize to Alex," she declared, turning and walking away, leaving Ivana to think on her words.

Ivana stood there, conflicted. She looked up and saw Alex in the distance, his back turned as he spoke with some workers. His presence brought back Sera's words, echoing in her mind. She really doesn't give a damn about what happens, but yet seeing Sera this way always aches her — Sera! And it will be best to just do what Sera wants.

Reluctantly, she approached him, her footsteps hesitant. When Alex noticed her, he seemed surprised but waited for her to speak.

"Alex," Ivana began, her voice cold. "I apologize for my earlier behavior. Your work is important, and it is appreciated."

Alex looked at her, raising an eyebrow. "I see, it's your nature to not give a damn."

He turned to walk away, but Ivana reached out and grabbed his hand, her grip firm. She hesitated, struggling with her pride and Sera's advice.

"Wait," she said, her voice softer now. "I... I'm sorry. Truly. Your contributions are valuable, and I respect the effort you've put in."

Alex paused, looking back at her. Her expression, though guarded, showed a hint of sincerity, or probably she was just faking it.

"Thank you, Your Majesty," he said, his tone more understanding. "It means a lot to hear that."

Ivana nodded slightly, letting go of his hand. "I'm trying to do what's best for the clan, even if it doesn't always seem that way. Your work is a crucial part of that effort."

Alex smiled, sensing a genuine shift in her tone. Seeing her like this felt quite strange, she was always high and mighty.

As Ivana walked away, she couldn't help but feel a bit lighter. Maybe, just maybe, she could balance her strength with a touch of empathy, but no matter how hard she tries, old habits die hard.

Ivana turned only to see Sera watching from afar, a proud smile on her face. Ivana couldn't help but smile back as she rolled her eyes. Sera always knew how to handle her stubbornness.

The showcase of the finished project felt like it took forever. Everyone was excited about it, but Ivana thought, "Seriously, it's just a fancy cart on train rails."

Later that evening, Ivana felt worn out. This queen's job wasn't easy, even after five years. The palace was hosting a big feast for Alex and his crew. Ivana wasn't completely happy about it. All this feasting would eventually eat into her sleep time, which she hadn't been getting enough of lately.

"My sleep!" Ivana sighed as she watched everyone gather around. "Ah! Why must it be today of all days?"

"Your Majesty?" Adrian called out as he approached.

"Adrian," she replied but her gaze seemed to be fix on a particular person.

"Your sleep, right?" Adrian declared, standing next to her and facing the feast.

"Wow, so it's that clear," she replied, almost surprised at how he guessed it.

"Well, I don't need to be smart to know that you value your sleep very much," he added with a smile.

Adrian couldn't help but notice how she kept looking at Alex, though her expression was rather difficult to read, every time Alex was close, her attention was always on him. He felt a pang of jealousy but tried to push it aside.

"Your Majesty," he ventured, "is something bothering you about Alex?"

Ivana glanced at Adrian, then back at Alex, again. She sighed. "He's competent, but he's not from our world. Sometimes, I wonder if he understands what's at stake here."

Adrian nodded, masking his own feelings. "He might surprise you. Sometimes, outsiders see things we usually miss."

Ivana considered his words. "Maybe. But I still don't have to like it."

Adrian forced a chuckle, though it pained him to say the words. "No, you don't. But at least give him a chance.

He might be more valuable than you think." His stomach churned with jealousy as the words left his mouth.

Ivana sighed, clearly tired of the topic. "Fine, but this feast better not last all night. I need my rest," she emphasized, her voice holding a note of finality. Adrian managed a small, quiet smile, though it was more from habit than happiness. He glanced over to see some old women trying to coax Alex into eating a dish that looked anything but appetizing.

Adrian hesitated, the question weighing heavily on his mind. Finally, unable to suppress his curiosity and jealousy, he took a risk. "Ivana, do you... do you like Alex?"

Ivana snapped her head towards him, her eyes narrowing. "What? No! Why would you even ask that?"

Adrian swallowed, his heart pounding. "I just thought... Never mind. It's just that you've been looking at him a lot tonight."

Ivana scoffed, her tone icy. "I look at everyone. It's part of my job as queen to observe."

Gathering his courage, Adrian pressed on, despite the weight of jealousy in his chest. "Well, if you don't like him, then maybe you could consider someone who's been by your side all these years."

For a brief moment, Ivana's expression softened, but her demeanor remained distant, she knew what message he was trying to relay. "Adrian, you're a good advisor, and I trust you. But don't overstep."

Adrian felt a pang of disappointment, though he wasn't entirely disheartened. "Understood, Your Majesty. But just so you know, I care about you. More than just an advisor should."

Ivana looked at him for a long moment, her eyes unreadable. "Adrian, your feelings are noted. But right now, I need to focus on leading this clan."

He nodded, a small flicker of hope still alive in his heart. "Of course, Your Majesty. I'll always be here for you."

Ivana turned her attention back to the feast, her expression unreadable. "Thank you, Adrian. Now, let's see how I'll survive tonight."

Just then, Sera approached Ivana, her eyes curious. "Ivana, they're waiting for you to join the feast," she said. "What were you discussing with Adrian?"

Ivana shrugged nonchalantly. "He confessed his love for me."

Sera's eyes widened in surprise. "And you just... tell me like that? Aren't you even a bit concerned about his feelings?"

Ivana waved her hand dismissively. "Concerned? Why should I be? All I want is sleep."

Sera sighed, shaking her head. "Ivana, seriously, will you ever like anyone?"

Ivana's expression remained unchanged. "Like I said, Sera, I just want to sleep."

Sera pressed gently, trying to reach her friend. "But don't you think it's important to let someone in? To let someone love you or to love someone back?"

Ivana looked at Sera with mild irritation. "Why does everyone keep pushing this? Love isn't a priority for me."

Sera placed a hand on Ivana's shoulder, her voice softening. "Ivana, you're a great queen, but ruling with only power and no heart will eventually isolate you. People need to feel that you care. You might not see it now, but allowing someone to get close could actually strengthen your reign, not weaken it."

Ivana frowned, her gaze drifting to the floor. "Maybe... but not now, Sera. Not now."

Sera sighed but gave Ivana a supportive smile. "Just think about it, okay? You deserve to be happy too, not just burdened with responsibility."

Ivana nodded, albeit reluctantly. "I'll think about it."

With that, Sera led her towards the feast, hoping that one day, Ivana would open her heart, even just a little.

Everyone gathered around the table, eager to start eating the mouth-watering dishes. Her arrival, as usual, was marked by an air of silent authority. Her expression still icy, she stood near her table, facing the others as she prepared to give an opening speech.

"Ladies and gentlemen," Ivana began, her voice steady and commanding. "Tonight, we celebrate the hard work and dedication that has brought us here. Let this feast be a reminder of our strength and unity."

The queen was always a source of amazement, a complex character that left people in awe. When she finished addressing the gathering, the applause was warm, yet she barely noticed. She took her seat, though her thoughts were elsewhere.

As she lifted her spoon, exhaustion crept in, followed by her old friend, Sleep, as if summoned by the mere act of eating. Ivana fought to stay awake, knowing that if she left the festival early, Sera would undoubtedly scold her. Trying her best to avoid dozing off, her gaze wandered around the room, eventually landing on Alex, who was mingling with the villagers. His easy link with the people, his genuine enthusiasm—it was both amusing and perplexing to her.

Meanwhile, Adrian's heart ached as he watched Ivana rise and walk toward Alex. He knew he couldn't change her feelings, but the sight still stung.

Ivana approached Alex, her steps measured and deliberate. Alex noticed her coming and excused himself from the conversation he was having, turning to face her with a mix of curiosity and apprehension, but she still felt something else, strange.

"Your Majesty," he greeted, bowing his head slightly.

Ivana looked at him, her expression as cold and unreadable as ever. "Alex," she acknowledged. "I see you're enjoying the festivities."

Alex nodded, unsure of her intentions. "Yes, Your Majesty. It's a wonderful celebration. The people are very grateful for your leadership."

Ivana tilted her head slightly, studying him. "And you, Alex? Are you grateful?"

He hesitated, then met her gaze. "Grateful..., sure I would have been dead if you hadn't saved me back then. But also confused. I don't understand why you keep me here."

Ivana sighed softly. "You have skills that are valuable to our clan. And, despite your reluctance, you've made significant contributions."

Alex looked around, feeling the weight of her words. "I suppose I have. But I can't help but feel like a pawn in a game I don't fully understand."

Ivana's eyes flickered with something unreadable. "Life is full of games, Alex. We all play our parts."

He frowned, frustrated by her cryptic response. "Is that all we are to you? Pieces on a board?"

She considered his question for a moment before responding. "Perhaps. But some pieces are more valuable than others."

Alex shook his head, a bitter smile on his lips. "I see. Well, I hope you find a way to win your game."

Ivana was about to respond when a guard came running, nearly crashing at her feet, panting heavily. She looked down at him, eyebrows slightly raised. "What's the matter?" she asked calmly.

"An army... thousands of men... they've camped right in front of the clan... preparing to attack us," the guard managed to say between breaths.

Ivana stayed calm, her face showing no sign of worry. Everyone around her looked scared, hoping she had a plan. She glanced up at the sky, almost as if asking why this was happening now. "Why today, why?" she muttered softly, thinking about how much sleep she was about to lose now.

Without another word, she teleported to the enemy camp. From a safe distance, she watched the soldiers. Torches lit up the area, casting shadows everywhere. Soldiers moved around, getting their weapons ready. The weapons looked different, more advanced and deadly. At first, she thought it was the kingdom of the north, but then she realized it was the east, from the royal stamp on their flags.

"You're in trouble now," she whispered to herself, recognizing the threat.

In an instant, she was back at the festival, where everyone waited anxiously for her return.

"What did you see?" Sera asked, her voice shaking. "How many are there?"

"Eighty-five thousand two hundred and sixty-three," Ivana replied casually, as if it was no big deal.

Sera fell to her knees, overwhelmed by the number. The crowd started murmuring in fear.

"What do we do?" Alex asked, his voice tight with worry.

"Nothing much," Ivana replied, waving Adrian over. "Seventy men only," she instructed. Adrian nodded, understanding completely, while Alex stared in disbelief. Seventy men to take down eighty thousand men, that is nearly impossible to balance, even if the queen is powerful.

"Wait, that few?" Alex blurted out, not believing what he heard.

"Yes, that few," Ivana repeated, sounding bored. "All of you, prepare to leave the clan just in case things get out of hand tomorrow."

Alex was stunned by how everyone seemed to take her word as law, showing no signs of panic. He watched as they began to follow her orders without hesitation. They all behaved like the ants to their queen, a social caste.

Ivana turned, her thoughts already drifting back to her interrupted rest. "If you'll excuse me, I need sleep," she said, walking calmly towards her chambers.

Adrian helped Sera to her feet. "It's amazing how she always stays calm," Sera said, a mix of admiration and concern in her voice.

"That's the queen for you," Adrian replied, respectful but resigned.

Alex stood there, marveling at the queen. Her calm attitude masked a mind always planning. The trust and respect she commanded were unlike anything he had ever seen. Despite the dire situation, he couldn't help but be amazed by her. Seventy men, that sounded like a bluff.

Chapter 11

Ivana lay in bed, surrounded by the stillness of the night, but sleep was elusive. Faint background noises filtered through the walls—probably Adrian, still awake. She tossed and turned, frustration building as her mind raced. The unknown intentions of the King of the East trouble her, and the mysterious dark figure only added to her unease. The thought of the King of the North potentially being involved made her feel even more unsettled. A kingdom as vast and powerful as the North was not something she could easily tackle.

Finally, she let out an exasperated growl, "Argh!" The tension was unbearable, and the questions of what lay ahead weighed heavily on her.

"Are you still awake?" Sera called quietly.

At first, Ivana didn't want to answer, but either way, she wasn't getting any sleep. "Come in."

Sera entered the room, a little surprised to see Ivana in an awkward position. She definitely wasn't sleeping. "I see even you couldn't sleep," Sera said, sitting close to her.

"It's just, I feel something's wrong," Ivana said, grabbing a pillow and hugging it tightly.

"What do you mean?"

"For starters, the King of the East knows he can't win against me. The destruction of other clans proves it, but he still declared war. This means he either has a plan or someone is backing him up."

Sera only smiled and said, "Irrespective, I know you. You always come up with a plan even against crazy odds."

"No, Sera," Ivana interjected. "I'm not telling you because I have a plan. I feel like something is off."

"Let me guess, you're afraid," Sera added.

"I'm not afraid of anything, you know that," Ivana replied, furious.

"Of course, that's why I'm not afraid either. That's why those seventy men will blindly follow you to that battle because they know you can turn everything upside down."

"No!" Ivana stressed. "Sera, this is something much bigger."

Sera only smiled as she gently pulled Ivana onto her lap, slowly rubbing her shoulder. "Ivana, I may not see the big picture, but the only piece of advice I can give you is don't be afraid. Be yourself."

Ivana sighed, disappointed that she didn't get the answer she was hoping for, but at least she knew Sera wasn't afraid. Eventually, sleep overtook her, and before she knew it, morning had arrived. She couldn't help but think it would have been better to attack the army at night, but the comfort of morning sleep was irresistible.

"Queen Ivana!" Adrian called repeatedly. "The enemy is advancing further in."

Ivana, barely awake, groggily stood up and opened the door to find Adrian, his face etched with concern. His expression shifted to one of surprise when he noticed the queen still wrapped in her nightgown, clutching a blanket like she had just rolled out of bed. Without a word, she brushed past him and made her way to the courtroom.

The room fell silent as everyone turned to see their queen. Her hair was in a mess, she was still in her nightgown, and her blanket trailed behind her, sweeping the floor.

"Your Majesty?" Thomas, the first elder, spoke up, his voice tinged with shock. "Isn't this too inappropriate?"

She sighed. "Didn't I try by coming quickly, or would you rather wait for me to get ready properly?"

"No, but..."

"Alright, Adrian, gather the men and head out. Wait for me at the entrance of the clan," she declared. "And bring Alex with you."

"Alex? But why?" Adrian questioned. "He doesn't have any experience in battle."

Ivana only glared at him, and with that expression, it was best to just do as she said.

"Sera, you and Thomas should gather the rest of the clan together and move out in the opposite direction of the enemy," Ivana added. "And the remaining men who aren't going to battle should protect everyone as you head out."

"What is your plan?" Adrian asked.

"Something fun," she said with a smile.

And just the same way she entered, she left, her blanket still sweeping the floor. Everyone dispatched according to the queen's orders.

The seventy men arrived at the entrance of the village. The entrance didn't have any fancy signs or gates to announce their presence. You would barely know it was there, except for a stone that had the name "Demon Clan" in their native language, carved into it.

They were overwhelmed by the sheer number of the enemy. The queen was not bluffing. You could hardly see their complete size, the woods hid their magnitude.

"Where is your beloved queen? Did she chicken out?" the enemy commander yelled, his men laughing with him.

"You should not mess with the power of the queen," Adrian shouted back, his men echoing his defiance.

"You guys should stop calling my name," the queen's voice echoed as she materialized from a dark cloud. She was dressed simply but elegantly, the teleportation particles settling around her.

"You're finally here," Adrian muttered. But the queen didn't respond, instead, she waved Alex to come closer.

Adrian still couldn't understand why they were getting closer. He knew the queen's personality and this wasn't like her.

"Is it ready?" she asked.

He nodded but quickly interjected, "Are you sure about this?"

"Alex, don't question, just do it."

He went to a bush and brought out a strange box with a lever and a long rope sticking out of it. Everyone was surprised and wondered what strange thing he had built this time.

The enemy began to charge towards them, the battle finally starting. Everyone was ready, but the queen didn't seem like she was going to take action yet.

"Now, your majesty?" Alex questioned, but she kept quiet as the enemy charged closer, until they reached an empty field.

"Alex, now!" she calmly declared.

With a pull of the lever, Alex set off a large explosion that killed many of the men at the front of the line. The rest were shocked and confused, trying to understand what had just happened.

The queen smiled as she looked at Alex, who was frozen by what he had just done.

"Alright, thanks, Alex," she said as she tied up her hair.

Dark veins began to appear around her face as her eyes turned black. She wasn't going to take it easy on the enemy army.

Almost instantaneously, she disappeared. A dark mist covered half of the enemy, and the only sounds were the cries of dying men. Just like that, nearly a quarter of the enemy was gone. Then, the skies turned darker and thunderclouds appeared.

It was terrifying how the queen summoned lightning. It struck nearly everywhere, except where Alex's bomb had exploded.

Alex couldn't believe what he was seeing. Although he had seen her in action before, this was beyond imagination. She was making the enemy look like they were the ones being attacked.

After several minutes of destruction, the queen finally dropped from the sky, blood trickling from her nose and ears. The thing about controlling lightning is that it also damages the caster, she can't really control lightning, it was just a special technique that tricked the natural appearance of it.

Seeing her, the enemy began to retreat, running back in fear. But the queen only waved at Alex, who pulled out a second lever and switched it. Immediately, a second explosion went off ahead of the enemy, stopping them in their tracks. They were terrified that if they kept moving, they might still die, seeing what the first explosion had done. They might not know how many are left hidden and unused.

"Alright, Adrian!" she called.

Understanding her, Adrian charged with the men, leaving Alex behind. The men, now with renewed morale from seeing the queen's power, pushed forward with vigor.

The battle continued, now a fierce and real clash between forces. The enemy, though large in number, was no match for the queen's relentless and strategic assault.

As the battle raged on, Ivana's forces steadily gained the upper hand. With the enemy's morale shattered by the queen's powerful display, they fell back in disarray. Adrian and his men pushed forward relentlessly, their spirits raised by Ivana's overwhelming power.

Eventually, the enemy's ranks broke completely, and the remnants of their army scattered, fleeing for their lives. The battlefield was littered with debris and fallen soldiers, a testament to the ferocity of the conflict.

Amidst the chaos, the enemy commander remained, his face twisted in defiance and fury. He was surrounded by a small group of his most loyal men, who stood their ground despite the odds. Ivana materialized in front of him, her presence commanding and terrifying.

"You fight well, but it's over," Ivana declared, her voice cold and unwavering.

The commander sneered. "You may have won this battle, witch, but the war is far from over. And you, Alex," he spat, turning his gaze to Alex, "how dare you help these demons? You betray your own kind for these monsters?"

Alex felt a surge of anger, firstly he was taken, it wasn't like he wanted to come here and secondly, wasn't he the same set of people together with the King that wanted him, but before he could respond, Ivana stepped forward, her eyes blazing with fury. "You dare insult my people?" she hissed.

The commander laughed bitterly. "Your people are nothing but savages, unworthy of the land they claim."

Without another word, Ivana lunged at the commander. They clashed in a blur of motion, their movements almost too fast to follow. Ivana's strikes were precise and deadly, each blow landing with bone-crushing force. The commander fought back fiercely, but it was clear he was outmatched.

Alex watched in awe and a hint of fear. He had seen Ivana's power before, but never this close, and never with such raw, terrifying intensity. Her eyes were filled with a cold, unrelenting rage that he had never seen before.

The commander, despite his skill, was no match for Ivana's fury. She moved with a grace and power that was almost supernatural, her every strike calculated to inflict maximum damage. The commander staggered back, bloodied and bruised, but he refused to yield.

"You and your clan will fall," he gasped, his voice filled with venom. "You cannot stand against the might of the East."

Ivana's expression hardened. "We shall see," she said quietly, and with one final, devastating blow, she sent the commander crashing to the ground.

He lay there, defeated and broken, his defiance extinguished. Ivana stood over him, her breathing steady, her gaze icy. "This is the fate of those who threaten my people," she said.

The battlefield fell silent, the weight of her words hanging in the air. The remaining enemies, seeing their leader defeated, dropped their weapons and surrendered, their will to fight completely shattered.

Ivana turned to Alex, her expression softening slightly. "Thank you for your help, Alex," she said, her voice almost gentle.

Alex nodded, still shaken by what he had witnessed. "I didn't realize... I didn't know you could...."

Ivana gave a small, grim smile. "There are many things you do not know about me, Alex. But for now, our clan is safe."

Adrian and the men gathered around, their faces filled with admiration and relief. "The battle is won, your majesty," Adrian said.

"Yes, it is," Ivana replied. She glanced at the sky, the dark clouds beginning to disperse. "Now, let's ensure our people are safe and tend to the wounded."

As they began to make their way back to the village, Alex couldn't help but glance at Ivana, his mind racing with questions. The terror he had seen in her eyes during the fight lingered in his thoughts, she is exactly what they said she was. She was a complex and formidable leader, one he was only beginning to understand.

The village erupted with cheers as news of the queen's victory spread. People embraced each other, relieved and joyous. The queen had once again proven her might, and the clan was safe.

"Tell the rest to return," Ivana declared, her voice firm. There was a hint of satisfaction in her usually stoic expression. It had been a long time since she had let out some steam, and those men had been unlucky.

Suddenly, the atmosphere shifted as a group of injured soldiers stumbled into the square. Their wounds were severe, and they looked shaken. Ivana's satisfaction quickly turned to concern.

"What happened?" she asked, her tone sharp.

One of the soldiers, barely able to stand, replied, "We were attacked by a strange smoke thing. He... he took Sera and... ran."

Ivana's heart sank, the feeling was strange but she didn't used to think about anything but now it's just, Sera. She knew exactly who the smoke thing was. Without a second thought, she sprinted away, her mind focused solely on rescuing Sera. She darted through the forest, her speed unmatched as she followed the faint trail left by the kidnapper. What exactly do they want with her? But it's going to pay if anything happens to Sera.

After what felt like an eternity, Ivana found them. The smoke man stood in a clearing, Sera bound and beaten at his feet. His face twisted into a sinister smile as Ivana approached, her fury barely contained.

"Hey, relax," the strange man taunted, his voice dripping with malice. "Don't do something stupid. Meet me in the East Kingdom, and we'll talk properly. But for now, I see you're exhausted from the battle."

Ivana's rage boiled over. She was ready to tear the world apart to save Sera. But before she could act, the smoke man vanished, taking Sera with him. His mocking laughter echoed through the trees, leaving Ivana standing there, disheartened and furious.

She clenched her fists, her mind racing. The thought of Sera in the hands of that monster was unbearable. She had to rescue her, no matter the cost. Ivana took a deep breath, forcing herself to stay calm. Panic would help no one.

Returning to the village, she found Adrian and Alex waiting. The worry in their eyes mirrored her own. Ivana didn't say a word. Her expression was unreadable as she walked past them and headed straight to her room.

Adrian and Alex exchanged worried glances but said nothing. They knew better than to push the queen when she was like this. The villagers, sensing something was wrong, fell silent as Ivana disappeared into the palace.

Once inside her room, Ivana collapsed onto her bed, burying her face in her hands. The weight of the situation pressed down on her. Sera was like a sister to her, and the thought of her in danger was almost too much to bear.

After a moment, she sat up, her resolve hardening. She couldn't afford to lose control. Sera needed her, and the clan depended on her strength. Ivana stood up, straightening her dress and wiping away any trace of vulnerability.

There was a knock at her door. Adrian entered, his face pale but determined.

"Your Majesty, what are your orders?"

Ivana took a deep breath. "Wait, just wait."

Adrian nodded, understanding the gravity of the situation. "As you wish."

As Adrian left without speaking further, Ivana looked out the window, her gaze fixed on the horizon. The smoke man had made a grave mistake by taking Sera. He would soon learn the true extent of her wrath.

Chapter 12

Adrian returned from the queen's room, his expression grim despite hearing what the queen said. He has never seen her like this, even though he can't tell what's reallying going on in her head. It is clear she is disheartened, if it was another person..., but it was Sera — Sera!.

"How is she holding up?" Thomas asked.

"All she said was, 'wait, just wait,'" Adrian sighed.

"Have you considered her? Do you think she can keep it together?"

"The queen?" Adrian tilted his head a bit. "Yes, but there's little to ponder. Whoever's behind this won't escape unscathed."

"Do you think she can confront them all with her demonic nature?"

"She could set the world ablaze if she wished. She's utterly relentless," Adrian replied.

Elder Thomas shook his head. "She always does this when she's angry. If she can't control something, she destroys it. It's both her strength and her weakness."

"Is the queen okay?" Alex asked, his worry evident. He approached the two discussing.

Adrian's expression changed, but he ignored the question.

Alex had been feeling increasing tension between him and Adrian. It wasn't like this before. He couldn't understand why Adrian was angry with him. He hadn't chosen to be involved in this conflict.

Feeling overwhelmed, Alex decided to leave the crowded courtroom and get some fresh air in the garden. As he walked, his mind raced with thoughts of finding a way to go back home, he had work diligently at the Clan and everyone praised him, their economic and their trades are now doing far better but still she refuse to at least acknowledge that she would let him return, what exactly does she want.

Unexpectedly, Alex came across Ivana as she was returning from the garden. Her expression was the same as any other day, as if nothing had happened—like she hadn't killed hundreds of men or lost Sera to kidnapping.

"Your Majesty!" Alex called out, hesitating slightly.

"Oh, Alex," she replied, her voice flat as she stopped and stared into his eyes. Her gaze was so intense it made his nerves stand on end.

"Are you alright?" he asked, trying to read her expression.

"Why wouldn't I be?" she replied nonchalantly.

"I mean, with Sera gone, it must be hard," Alex said, his voice tinged with concern.

"Hard? For me?" she scoffed. "There will always be a replacement for Sera."

Alex couldn't believe his ears, how could she just say that, only a few weeks in the Clan everyone told him that she really adored Sera but yet, she is really heartless. But what unsettled him more was the way she was staring at him—intently, as if probing his very soul.

"Is there something wrong?" Alex asked, his voice faltering.

"Alex, who are you?" she asked suddenly, her tone cold and calculating.

"What do you mean?" he stammered.

"I find it strange how we met at the marketplace, and coincidentally, you turned out to be an economic expert. Strangely enough, the king was able to locate us back when they tried to arrest us. There's no way they could have known where this place is unless someone told them."

"What are you saying?" Alex stammered, his fear rising. "Why would I do that? Aren't you the one who brought me here?"

"I can go from nice to evil in the next few seconds, so answer me sincerely," she replied, her expression still nonchalant. It was impossible to tell if she was joking.

"I don't know what you're talking about," he replied coldly, trying to mask his fear.

"Alex!" she yelled suddenly, her voice echoing with power. "I can make you feel things you can't unfeel." An invisible force struck him, sending him sprawling to the ground, blood spurting from his mouth. "Take this as a warning. You better start talking," she said calmly, as if nothing had happened.

Alex struggled to his feet, his body trembling. "I'm done. I can't take this anymore," he declared, turning to leave. Fear coursed through his veins, but he knew she could kill him at any moment.

"Do you want to die?" she threatened. "Do you want your family to die?"

He stopped in his tracks, fists clenched at his sides. Then, he turned back toward her, a bitter smile on his lips. "You know, when you can't control something, you threaten to kill it. And if it doesn't obey, it dies," he said, his voice breaking with emotion.

He wiped the blood from his mouth, staring into the clouds. "Do you know why I stayed and did everything you asked?" he said, his voice softer now. "It was for one person, Sera."

"I don't care if you burn me straight to hell. Maybe everyone here trusts you, and maybe you have all these powers. But remember that first day we met at the market? I didn't help you because I knew you were the queen. I helped you because I thought you needed it."

"I never asked for your help," she replied, her voice devoid of emotion.

He sighed heavily as he looked at her smiling at bit. "How do you always do it? Keep your emotions and expressions nonchalant. I've got to know."

"Your Majesty, that day we met, I took a liking to you. But once I found out you were the Demon Queen, I tried to convince myself that maybe I might still like you and Sera made me believe that That's why I agreed to stay. But now I realize it's just your nature. You can't help it."

"I'm leaving tomorrow. If you have anything to say to me, you have until then," Alex declared, turning his back on her and walking away.

Ivana stood there in silence, her expression unchanging as she absorbed his words. For the first time in a long while, something seemed to stir within her, but she quickly pushed it down, retreating back into her cold, heartless facade.

Ivana watched Alex quietly as he slowly walked away. There was something about him that didn't sit right with her—a feeling that he wasn't what he seemed, it felt familiar but she just can't put her teeth on it.

"Your Majesty!" Elder Thomas called as he approached the scene. Ivana's eyes widened abit, realizing he might have witnessed the confrontation.

"Is there a problem?" she asked calmly.

"Not really," he replied, gesturing for her to take a seat on one of the garden benches. "Let's talk."

After sitting down, Ivana couldn't help but ask, "How much did you see?"

"With Alex? Well, everything," he replied slowly. "But why were you two arguing?"

"Nothing. I was just interrogating him," she said.

"So, he's a suspect already," Thomas smiled. "Will I also become a suspect too?"

Those words finally caught Ivana's attention. She looked rather surprised by his insinuation.

"Why are you surprised? I might be a spy, or worse, I might have instigated everything that has happened," he declared.

She scoffed. "I know you. You wouldn't do such a thing. That's why I made you the first elder." He burst into laughter, clapping his hands. "Wow, so you know me, but you don't know Alex, which is why you suspect him."

"I am not that irrational," Ivana retorted. "If you don't have something to say, I have a lot of work."

"Calm down, Your Majesty. There's no reason to get serious," he said, raising his hands in a placating gesture. "Your mother, Ivana the Second, was—"

Before he could finish, she interjected, her rage evident. "Hey, I warned all of you not to mention her name in my presence, ever."

"Sorry," he replied, his tone sadden as he recalled everything that had transpired between the queen and her mother. "But there's something she said: 'Ivana will be the most powerful queen in the world, but she will not understand the essence of human nature.' At first, it seemed like a curse, but it wasn't. It was just an observation of you when you were small."

Ivana didn't find anything of value in what he was saying, so she stood to leave without consideration.

"You see, you did it again—human nature," he declared as she stopped slowly in her tracks.

"Now, let's talk about Sera. How does she feel being taken away from her clan by a powerful person?" he continued. "She can't fight him or do anything. She might as well be his slave already. Just imagine the things she might be going through, being far from her family and friends."

"How is that my problem? There will always be a replacement for her," Ivana turned to face him and declared nonchalantly.

"You did it again—human nature," he called out. "Let me guess, because you can't be replaced but, unfortunately for all of us pawns, we can be, right?"

She lowered her head a little, calmly muttering, "She will be fine. They won't dare lay a finger on her."

He stood up and got closer to her. "Alex—you brought him here against his will."

"Well, I couldn't let him be killed back there," she replied.

"Yes, of course. Let's say you did care back there. But no, you saved him because you knew he would have nowhere to go but to serve you," he said.

He patted her shoulder. "Your Majesty, the same way Sera is feeling now is the same way Alex has been feeling all along. He can't rival the great queen of the demon clan. All he can do is obey you and pray that one day you will let him go back. Unlike you, he shows he cares about his family."

"Alex—I don't care how he feels. All I care about is the clan growing," she said, removing his hand from her shoulder and scoffing. "Thus, your words mean nothing to me. Absolutely nothing."

He sighed. "You did it again. Stop forcing them away. No matter how hard you hide those feelings, one day they will surface, and it won't be great."

"Thomas!" she yelled. "Don't forget who you are talking to."

"Of course, I haven't forgotten," he replied, his voice calm yet firm, he smiled a bit as he walked away, Ivana stood quietly, taking in his words. The garden around her seemed eerily still, reflecting the turmoil inside her. She clenched her fists, trying to suppress the emotions Thomas's words had stirred. For the first time in a long while, she felt a pang of doubt, wondering if she had indeed lost touch with the very essence of human nature, it feels contradicting..., and she doesn't like it.

Later that night, Ivana found herself pacing in her chambers. The moonlight streamed through the window, casting long shadows that mirrored her conflicted state of mind. Her thoughts raced, replaying the confrontation with Alex and Thomas's piercing insights. She wanted it to stop, but the more she tried, the more it reoccurred.

She sat down at her desk, absentmindedly tracing her fingers over an old, worn map of her kingdom. Memories of her mother surfaced—Ivana the Second, a queen who had wielded power with both compassion and an iron fist, or so they thought. Everyone knew how much she hated her mother, but nobody knew why, a secret only between them. Her mother's legacy loomed large, a constant reminder of what Ivana could be but often chose not to be.

Ivana's gaze drifted to a small locket on her desk, a relic from her childhood. She opened it, revealing a faded picture of her and her mother. "Ivana will be the most powerful queen in the world but she will not understand the essence of human nature." Thomas's words echoed in her mind. Was she truly living up to that prophecy? "I hate you!" she yelled as she threw the locket so hard that it broke. She sighed deeply.

A knock on the door broke her reverie. It was a maiden, one of Sera's attendants. Ivana never seemed to catch any of their names. The maid's face was a mixture of concern and fear. "Your majesty, is everything alright?"

Ivana's expression changed back to its usual calm as she turned to face her. "I'm fine. Just thinking."

"About Sera?" the maid ventured carefully, unable to hide the fear in her voice. She was actually shaking. But Ivana wasn't in the mood to deal with another person.

"And other things," Ivana replied, her tone nonchalant but her eyes betraying a deeper turmoil.

The maid hesitated before speaking again. "If I may, your majesty, if you want to talk about anything, I am here to listen."

"Listen?" Ivana scoffed, though her voice lacked its usual edge. "Wait, who are you first?"

"I am the maid directly under Sera. I was to take over if anything happens to her," she declared.

"Her replacement," Ivana said, a cold smile touching her lips. "Sera assigned her own replacement."

"You might remember me. On my very first day, you tried to kill me because I didn't contradict my answers," the maid reminded her.

"Oh, yeah, I remember. I told you I had gained weight," Ivana added. "Oh, you have really grown." It had actually been a few months ago, but Ivana hardly remembers any of the maids or servants; they were always new ones here and there.

The room went silent until the queen spoke again. "Since what I did to you, are you still afraid of me?"

Hesitant at first, the maid replied, "I did fear you before and even hated you a little, but Sera encouraged me and showed me how to see the good side in you. But even though I tried, I couldn't help but feel fear in your presence. Even right now, I can't help myself; my body wants to run away but fear is holding me."

Ivana stood up and moved closer to the maid. It was as if hell stood close to her. Ivana watched her closely. "You are afraid of me, but then why did you choose to stay or yet come here to talk to me?"

The maid stammered, her fear evident. "Well... because I wanted to help you."

"That's not the answer I wanted to hear," Ivana replied coldly as she pushed her to the wall. It was like the very first time. The maid thought she couldn't help but cry; tears ran down her cheeks. The demeanor and aura of the queen were frightening.

"I will ask you one more time. Why did you come to meet me?" Ivana asked, pressing her shoulder harder into the wall.

"I just wanted to help!" the maid emphasized, but it wasn't getting through to the queen.

"Fine!" At that moment, the queen's eyes turned black. It was evident that she was going to do something terrible to her. The maid was at her mercy. Ivana increased the pressure on her.

"Stop! Please stop!"

Strangely enough, Ivana snapped back, seeing the vulnerability in the maid. Only to realize she had injured the maid as she bled.

"Ah!" the maid screamed. Seeing what she had done, Ivana realized she had gone too far as she staggered back, her eyes filled with fear, she slowly sat down on the ground, it had only been hours since Sera was taken and she was already falling apart.

"Wait, please, your majesty, calm down," the maid entreated despite being injured. "I don't want you to feel bad about this."

"Why?" Ivana asked, surprised.

"Like I said, I came here to help you. Whether you beat me up or not, as long as it makes you feel better, I will do it. Only Sera understands you. I can't ever compare to her, but I can try," the maid explained as she walked closer to the queen, who was sitting on the floor.

The maid came and squatted and slowly hugged her. "I only want to help you." Ivana could sense the fear in the maid but to see her try, just try, it made her feel even more bad.

"I am sorry," Ivana said, the words were heavy, it felt like it wanted to draw everything from her out, as tears gathered in her eyes, barely trying to hold it in. For the first time in a long while, Ivana burst into tears right in front of the maid, embracing her tightly. It took some moment as the room went silent only the two, Ivana feeling conflicted and the maids heart pounding slowly.

After the maid left, Ivana sat in silence, absorbing everything that had transpired. The weight of her responsibilities pressed down on her, but so did the possibility of change. She rose and walked to the window, looking out over her kingdom. The night was quiet, but her mind was anything but. She needs to make something right, first.

In the early hours of the morning, Ivana made her decision. She summoned Alex to her chambers, her expression still unreadable. Alex entered cautiously, clearly wary but with a glimmer of hope in his eyes. "You called for me, your majesty?"

"Yes," Ivana said, her voice steady. "We're going to the east."

Alex blinked in surprise. "What? Why?"

"I have my reasons," she replied, her tone nonchalant as ever, but there was a slight tremor in her voice that she couldn't quite hide. "It's a strategic decision."

Alex searched her face for any hint of her true intentions, but she remained difficult. "Thank you," he said cautiously.

"Don't thank me yet, I can change my mind anytime," she replied. "This is not for you." Ivana knew something had truly changed within her.

As Alex left to prepare for the journey, Ivana stood alone, staring at the broken locket once more. Her mother's image seemed to watch over her, a silent reminder of the legacy she carried.

"I am going to prove you wrong. Just you wait, mother."

Chapter 13

It had been almost a year working with the demon clan, Alex thought as he packed up the few belongings he'd managed to gather. He hadn't exactly been kidnapped with all his stuff. Getting used to life here has been a challenge. The daily activities were unlike anything he'd known; sometimes it felt like he was living among entirely different beings. But thanks to Sera, he had managed to sneak letters to his family, always risking the wrath of the queen if she ever found out.

Walking through the bustling streets, Alex reminisced about all the strange and wonderful things he'd built in the town. His handiwork was everywhere. The newly laid rail tracks gleamed under the sunlight, a testament to his efforts. He still marveled at how quickly the project had come together; a task that should have taken years had taken only three months. It felt surreal to be so integrated into the clan, to live freely among them—even with the queen watching his every move. He chuckled at the thought of returning home without a good explanation; his mother would surely have his head. "Home," he mused, almost wistfully.

"Ah," the queen's voice cut through his thoughts, pulling him back to the present. "Don't tell me you're about to cry."

"Of course not," he replied quickly, though his voice wavered. She raised an eyebrow, clearly skeptical. "It's just... I'm going to miss this place."

"What's wrong with you? Weren't you the one begging me to let you go?" she shot back. Alex just smiled as a group of his workers came running over.

"Alex, we're going to miss you!" they shouted, enveloping him in a group hug. The queen took this as her cue to step aside, finding a quiet corner from which to watch.

"Please don't go, we need you here," one of the younger men pleaded. Alex couldn't help but laugh, his eyes widening. They wanted him to stay? It was almost funny, considering how he never intended to work here in the first place. "I've taught you everything I know," he replied, "Now it's up to you to keep building and make this place even better."

The small gathering quickly grew into a crowd, everyone eager to bid Alex farewell. They brought gifts and tokens of appreciation—so many that he'd have a hard time carrying them all. It was touching to see how he'd won over the hearts of so many, from the youngest to the oldest in the clan.

The queen, watching the scene unfold, felt a twinge of impatience. She had no plans to use her teleportation powers, meaning the journey to the East would take weeks. But if they didn't leave soon, these villagers might convince Alex to stay. Growing frustrated, she shouted, "Hey! Alex, let's go."

"Can't you wait a little longer?" Alex called back with a smile, but the look on the queen's face made it clear she was not amused. Her glare was answer enough.

Finally breaking away from the crowd, they began their long journey. Alex couldn't help but wonder why the queen chose not to teleport. Although his first experience with teleportation had been less than pleasant, it might have saved them weeks of travel.

That night, as they set up camp, Alex watched the fish he caught roast over the fire. He noticed the queen staring at him, not in her usual indifferent way, but almost as if she were searching for something. What exactly, he had no idea.

The silence was heavy, so he decided to break it. "You've been quiet this whole journey. Is something on your mind?" She didn't answer. He was getting used to that.

"Alright, I think they're ready," he said, offering her some fish. She looked at it skeptically.

He chuckled. "Oh, let me guess. You think I poisoned it?"

She gave him a look, then grabbed the fish and, with a flick of her wrist, set it aflame with her powers. "I need to sleep," she muttered, turning away to lie down. Alex stared at the burnt fish and sighed. Just a few more days, and he'd be free of her.

"Right," he muttered to himself, settling by the fire. He looked up at the starry sky, feeling a strange peace. It had been a while since he'd camped out like this.

The next morning, Alex woke to find the queen still asleep. He'd heard stories about how she'd skip important meetings just to catch up on sleep, but seeing her sleep so soundly in the wilderness was something else. It was almost... peaceful. He almost felt guilty for having to wake her.

"Hmm, look how peaceful she looks," he muttered quietly. "But she's a monster inside."

Seeing that the sun was climbing higher, he knew they needed to get moving. He reached out to wake her, but before he could touch her, she mumbled, "Touch me, and I will burn you."

"Ah, you're awake."

"Stop talking and let's continue our journey," she grumbled, still half-asleep.

Alex shook his head, amused. "I'm ready, but you're the one still trying to sleep." She simply ignored him, and he chuckled to himself, knowing this journey was far from over.

It had been nearly a week since they set out, and they hadn't even covered half the distance. The road seemed to stretch on endlessly, each mile disappearing into the next. Alex was tired—no, exhausted. This was his first time traveling so far, and not even his master, Maxymn, had prepared him for a journey like this. Worse still was the company: a heartless woman who wouldn't stop at any of the towns they passed, not even for a moment of rest.

He watched as yet another town slipped by into the horizon. "How can anyone be so heartless?" he muttered under his breath, frustration tightening his grip on the reins. "Ah!" he growled louder, the sound echoing in the empty road.

"Your Majesty," he called out, raising his voice over the wind, "can't we just stop and eat something decent? Sleep on a comfortable bed for a change?" But she wasn't listening. Or if she was, she didn't care.

Alex turned to look back at the disappearing town, fading into the distance. "C'mon, seriously, what's your problem?" he shouted again, but she continued ahead, her back straight, her posture unwavering.

Finally, he'd had enough. Frustrated and on the verge of boiling over, Alex yanked the reins, bringing his horse to a sudden halt. "I'm not going any further until you explain why you're acting like this!"

Ivana stopped her horse as well, turning slowly to face him. Her expression was unreadable, a mask of calm indifference, but her eyes—her eyes were something else entirely. They bore into him with a cold, distant intensity that sent a chill down his spine.

"I don't understand you," Alex continued, his voice rising. "I know you're taking me back to my home, but you barely say a word and refuse to stop even for a moment. Not everyone is as relentless as you!"

Still, Ivana remained silent, her gaze never wavering, like a hawk watching its prey.

"Why won't you say anything?" he shouted, his frustration spilling over like a dam breaking. "What is your problem? Are you really this heartless?"

Ivana's face remained nonchalant, her eyes narrowing just slightly. "Enough," she said, her voice dangerously low.

But Alex was too far gone to care. "No, it's not enough!" he snapped. "I deserve some answers! Why are you like this? Why do you treat everyone around you like they're nothing?"

There was a tension in the air now, thick and palpable. Her patience snapped. In a blur of motion, she unsheathed her sword and lashed out. Before Alex could react, the blade had pierced his left hand with cold, ruthless precision.

He gasped, a sharp cry of pain escaping his lips as he clutched his bleeding hand. Blood trickled down his fingers, staining the ground below.

Ivana pulled back her sword, her eyes still locked onto his with that same cold detachment. "You do not question me," she said icily. "You do not demand answers from me."

Alex fell to his knees, pain coursing through him, his breath coming in ragged gasps. He looked up at her, anger and confusion twisting his features. "Why?" he managed to choke out. "Why do you have to be like this?"

"I am only taking you back to your land," she replied, her tone cold as steel. "I am not here to bond with you. Leave it at that." She moved closer, her eyes darkening, the tip of her sword just inches from his chest. "Complain again, and I will do more than injure you."

For a moment, her mask slipped. There was a flicker of something in her eyes—something that almost looked like regret—but it was gone as quickly as it appeared. "Get up," she ordered, her voice sharp. "We're continuing the journey."

Alex staggered to his feet, the pain in his hand throbbing with each beat of his heart. His mind raced, and for a moment, his frustration slipped, revealing a hint of something else—a strength, a resolve that was just beneath the surface. He quickly masked it, but Ivana's eyes narrowed. She sensed something, a shift in his demeanor.

He tried to play it off, forcing a smile despite the pain. "Fine," he said, his voice steady, but there was a slight tremor in it. "I guess, I should know my place. Right?."

Ivana's suspicion had been growing for a while now. There was something about Alex—something he was hiding. She couldn't put her finger on it, but there was a sense of mystery around him that kept her on edge. For now, though, she chose to keep her thoughts to herself, watching and waiting.

As Alex mounted his horse, he heard the sudden sound of hurried footsteps. Before he could react, a young woman burst out from the nearby trees, her eyes wide with fear. Without thinking, Alex jumped down from his horse and approached her, noticing the way her whole body trembled.

"Are you alright?" he asked softly, trying to ease her fear with his calm tone.

The woman's eyes darted around, searching the shadows behind her. She opened her mouth to speak but no words came out; fear had stolen her voice.

Moments later, several men emerged from the trees, their faces twisted into menacing grins. Ivana glanced at them, recognizing their type instantly—predators who thrived on the fear of others. She had seen their kind before and felt a flicker of anger. She dismounted her horse with a quiet grace, her expression darkening.

The men, seeing Alex and Ivana, seemed amused, completely unaware of the danger they were in.

The man in front, smirking as he stepped forward, said, "Hand over the girl, and no one gets hurt." He paused, eyeing

Ivana up and down with a sleazy grin. "And maybe you can join her, make it a good time for us."

Ivana's eyes flashed with a cold, steely look. "You think you can make demands of me?" she asked, her voice low and sharp.

The men laughed, dismissing her with a wave. "Who do you think you are, lady?" another man taunted. "This is our territory. Move aside, now."

Without a word, Ivana's hand moved to her sword, and in one fluid motion, she drew it and slashed, cutting through the air with deadly precision. The first man didn't even have time to scream before he fell to the ground, clutching his chest.

The sudden attack stunned the others for a moment, but they quickly regrouped, readying themselves to fight. Alex, despite the pain in his injured hand, felt a surge of determination. He wasn't about to let these men hurt anyone. He stepped in, swinging his weapon, knocking one of the attackers to the ground.

Ivana moved through the group like a shadow, each swing of her sword finding its mark. Her movements were swift, controlled, and lethal. The men barely had time to register what was happening before they were on the ground, groaning in pain or worse.

Alex fought with a quiet intensity, every strike carrying a hint of something more—a strength that seemed almost unnatural. Ivana noticed it too, watching him out of the corner of her eye. There was something about the way he moved, a hidden power he was trying to conceal. It only made her more suspicious.

Within moments, the fight was over. The men lay scattered on the ground, defeated. The young woman, still trembling, looked at Ivana with wide eyes, a mix of fear and gratitude shining in them. "Thank you," she whispered, her voice barely audible.

Ivana cleaned her sword with a swift motion, her face unreadable. "Find somewhere safe," she said, her tone firm but not unkind. Without waiting for a response, she turned back to her horse, mounting it in one smooth motion.

As she settled back into her saddle, her eyes flicked back to Alex. He was still breathing hard, wiping sweat from his brow, but there was something in his posture—something almost... powerful. It made her uneasy. He was hiding something, she was sure of it. And whatever it was, she was determined to find out.

Alex climbed back onto his horse, trying to ignore the queen's piercing gaze. He could feel her watching him, studying him like a puzzle she couldn't quite solve. He forced a smile, masking the turmoil inside.

"Wait," the woman said, her voice trembling with desperation. "Please, help me. My sister and other women are being held captive in the next town. I escaped, but they couldn't. You have to help them."

Ivana let out an impatient sigh. "We've done enough. She can take care of herself now."

Alex shook his head firmly. "No, she's clearly terrified. We can't just leave her or the others behind like this."

Ivana's eyes flashed with irritation. "And what exactly do you propose we do? We have a journey to finish."

"We can't ignore this," Alex pressed. "We have to help them."

Ivana crossed her arms, her gaze hardening. "I don't have time for this."

Alex held his ground, meeting her glare. "Maybe you don't, but I do. If you're so heartless that you can't see these women need help, then maybe I've been wrong about you all along."

For a moment, they stood locked in a tense silence. Ivana's eyes narrowed, sizing him up, but Alex didn't flinch. Finally, she rolled her eyes and turned away.

"Fine," she said with a dismissive wave. "Do whatever you want. But don't expect me to hold your hand through it."

Alex smiled, grateful for the small victory. "Thank you, Your Majesty. I'll make sure they're safe."

"Wait, you're bleeding," the woman pointed out, noticing a wound on Alex's hand.

He winced slightly but then smirked. "Had a run-in with a nasty monster this morning. Managed to get a swipe in."

"Monster? Really?" the woman asked, surprised by his casual tone.

"Monster, indeed." Ivana's eyes bored into him, a sly smile tugging at her lips. "I hope it doesn't come back to finish the job."

Alex laughed nervously at her words, while the young woman, unaware of the hidden tension, looked between them, confused.

"Can we move on?" Ivana yawned. "I'm feeling sleepy."

They set off toward the next town, the young woman riding alongside Alex. As they rode, Alex couldn't help but feel a sense of accomplishment. He'd managed to break through Ivana's tough exterior, if only a little. But he knew the challenge wasn't over yet. The real test was still ahead. What was he thinking? He doesn't know why he is doing this, he should let the sleeping dogs lie but he just finds her interesting, the mystery, the enigma. He wants to know who Ivana the Third is.

The town wasn't far from where they had met the young woman, tucked away in dense vegetation. It was the kind of place you could pass without noticing, hidden and quiet. Ivana rode ahead, her posture stiff with irritation. Agreeing to help had not been part of her plan, and she knew Alex would relish in this small victory. She decided then and there—he would pay for this later.

As they entered the town, it seemed almost too normal. People moved about their business—stall owners calling out for customers, travelers resting under shaded awnings. The scent of fresh bread mingled with the earthy smell of the nearby forest, and the sounds of merchants haggling filled the air. It was hard to imagine anything sinister lurking here.

"Let's find a place to stay and come up with a plan," Alex suggested as they walked through the bustling streets, his voice tinged with anticipation.

Ivana cut her eyes towards him, her face betraying none of her thoughts. "There's no need for that. Let's find those criminals and leave," she replied, her tone as cold as the steel of her blade.

Alex sighed, sensing her growing frustration. "Just one night. I promise, no more complaints for the rest of the journey."

Ivana clenched her jaw, her gaze sweeping over the townspeople with suspicion. The thought of staying in a place where she could be recognized didn't sit well with her. If anyone discovered she was the Demon Queen, it could mean trouble—more than she cared to deal with.

Before she could object further, a well-dressed man stepped out from a doorway, his face bright with a welcoming smile. "Ah, travelers! Looking for a place to rest?"

"Yes!" Alex responded eagerly, almost too quickly.

"No!" Ivana shot back, her voice sharp enough to cut.

The man hesitated, looking between them. "Well... is it a yes or a no?"

"Yes, don't mind her," Alex said quickly, stepping closer to the man and lowering his voice to a conspiratorial whisper. "She's just a bit... particular about our route. We've been traveling across the Big South, and she's not happy we've changed directions."

The man chuckled, clearly amused. "Ah, a lover's quarrel? Are you two newlyweds?" he asked with a wink.

Without missing a beat, Alex nodded. "Yes, we're on our honeymoon."

Ivana's eyes flared with shock and anger. "What did you just say?"

Alex felt her gaze like a knife in his back, but he forced a smile. He knew he was stepping into dangerous territory, but seeing her caught off guard was worth it. Just a little bit of payback for all her coldness.

The man, oblivious to the tension, clapped his hands together. "Wonderful! You've come to the right place. Our inn is perfect for a romantic stay. You'll love it."

Ivana's eyes narrowed, her lips pressed into a thin line. "We are leaving," she said icily, her tone leaving no room for argument.

Alex, emboldened by his small victory, stood his ground. "No, we're staying. And that's final."

For a moment, the air between them crackled with unspoken threats. Ivana stared down at him, her eyes burning with a mix of anger and something else—something Alex couldn't quite place. Then, a slow, cold smile spread across her face, sending a shiver down his spine.

"You will regret this," she said softly, her voice like velvet over steel.

Alex's faltered slightly. "What do you mean?"

Ivana turned to the innkeeper with a sweet smile that didn't reach her eyes. "We'll take the most expensive room you have," she said, her tone saccharine yet deadly. "My husband here will pay for it."

Alex blinked, his mouth opening and closing like a fish out of water. "The most expensive? Who's paying?"

Ivana's eyes glinted with amusement. "You, of course," she said smoothly. "Who else?"

Alex stammered, but Ivana had already dismissed him, turning her attention back to the inn. "Hey, you, let's go," she called to the young woman, her voice firm and commanding.

Alex had no choice but to follow, feeling the weight of the situation bearing down on him. The inn was small but cozy, with warm lighting and the faint scent of lavender in the air. The innkeeper led them up a narrow staircase to a spacious room with a large bed covered in fine linens.

Alex could feel the heat of Ivana's anger radiating off her. He swallowed hard, knowing he had crossed a line. As the door closed behind them, he braced himself for what was to come.

"Did you have to go that far?" Alex sighed, his voice heavy with frustration.

Ivana turned to him, a cold smile playing on her lips. "Why, husband, aren't you supposed to pay the bills?" she replied, her tone mockingly sweet.

Alex clenched his fists, fighting back the urge to argue. He pointed a finger at her, but instead of speaking, he just shook his head and slumped onto one of the couches.

After settling in, Alex caught Ivana's gaze lingering on his injured hand, still oozing blood from the earlier fight. She tossed a cloth in his direction without a word, her expression unreadable.

"What's this for?" Alex asked, confusion furrowing his brow.

"For your hand," she said, nodding toward his injury.

"Oh, right," he mumbled, suddenly aware of the stinging pain. "I almost forgot."

She raised an eyebrow, her skepticism evident. "You... forgot?"

Alex managed a faint smile as he wrapped the cloth around his hand. "I knew you weren't completely heartless."

Ivana scoffed, her eyes narrowing. "Don't get used to it. Next time, you're on your own."

Alex chuckled softly, shaking his head. Beneath her hardened exterior, he sensed a different side of Ivana—a side she wasn't ready to reveal. He was determined to see it, even if it meant pushing his luck.

As they prepared for the night, the young woman they had rescued earlier approached them hesitantly, her eyes clouded with guilt. "I'm sorry for interrupting your journey. I didn't realize you two were on your honeymoon."

Ivana opened her mouth to correct her, but Alex quickly cut in. "Don't worry about it," he said, his tone light. "My wife and I enjoy taking on dangerous missions. Adds a bit of excitement to our honeymoon, don't you think?"

Ivana shot him a glare that could melt steel. "Alright, I am definitely going to kill you."

The young woman's face brightened, though still laced with uncertainty. "Thank you... for everything. I'm truly grateful."

Alex nodded, stepping closer, his eyes soft with understanding. "Really, it's no trouble. We couldn't just leave those people behind, right?"

Ivana's gaze bore into him, her silence heavy with contemplation. Finally, she let out a resigned sigh. "Fine. But if this turns out to be a waste of time, you'll regret it."

Alex's smile widened, sensing a small victory. "Thank you."

"But I'm taking the bed," she declared, dropping onto the soft mattress with a satisfied sigh.

"Wait, what about us?" Alex protested, glancing between her and the young woman.

Ivana's smirk was almost playful. "You can sleep on the floor. She can have the couch."

The young woman quickly shook her head. "Oh, no, please. I'll sleep on the floor. I don't want to impose."

Ivana waved her hand dismissively. "No, Alex loves sleeping on the floor. Says soft surfaces hurt his back." She grinned at him, her eyes gleaming with mischief.

Alex's jaw tightened, but he forced a tight smile. "Right... I guess I had that coming," he muttered under his breath.

As they settled in for the night, the tension between Alex and Ivana simmered, but he couldn't help feeling a growing determination. Despite their differences, they were in this together, and he was starting to see a hint of something more beneath her cold facade—a spark of humanity she kept buried deep. He was determined to uncover it, no matter how many times she tried to push him away.

Ivana lay on the bed, staring at the ceiling, her mind racing with the events of the past few days. She couldn't shake the frustration gnawing at her. Alex had managed to get under her skin in a way she hadn't anticipated. He had a knack for pushing her buttons, and now she found herself questioning why she had agreed to stay in the town.

Her thoughts were consumed by the urgency to find Sera. She knew that every wasted moment could mean more danger for her sister and the others. Yet, here she was, tangled in an unexpected detour.

Ivana sighed heavily, feeling the weight of her frustration and the cost of Alex's persistence. It had been a long time since anyone had managed to provoke such a reaction from her. If it were up to her, Alex would have faced a much harsher fate by now.

Turning her head slightly, she glanced down at Alex, who lay peacefully on the floor, the soft rise and fall of his chest the only indication of his presence. For a moment, Ivana's steely resolve wavered. Why couldn't she remain completely indifferent? Why did his stubbornness and persistence affect her so deeply?

If she were in her usual mood, Alex would have faced a far different outcome. Her nature was to remain unyielding, to keep her emotions locked away and her decisions uncompromising. She couldn't pinpoint exactly what, but his constant attempts to draw her into conversation had made her more reflective than she was accustomed to.

It wasn't just his demeanor that intrigued her; there was something unsettling about him. Normal humans emitted a certain frequency of energy, a kind of static hum that was easy to gauge. But Alex's energy was strikingly low—almost imperceptible. It was as though he was hiding something profound beneath his surface, something he wasn't willing to reveal. It made her uneasy, a silent alarm that something was wrong.

He was irritating, much like Sera in some ways, yet there was a difference she couldn't quite place.

Ivana's thoughts drifted, the exhaustion of the day catching up with her. She allowed herself a small, wistful smile, recognizing the irony of her situation. Here she was, caught between duty and an unexpected, irritating connection with someone who seemed to defy her usual expectations.

Closing her eyes, she surrendered to the encroaching darkness, allowing the weariness to pull her under. The weight of her responsibilities and the lingering thoughts of Alex slowly faded into the shadows of her mind.

Chapter 14

You could just imagine the pain of sleeping on the floor after paying for a queen-sized bed. She couldn't even cover the entire bed but was completely territorial over it. Maybe she should have allowed the young woman. All this he thought of as the young woman guided them to a strange storehouse, his eyes affixed on the queen. He just couldn't help it again, he knows he is pushing his luck, but anything now to really see the real Ivana, how will she react if she found out who he really was. It had large windows high on the walls and a massive main door. The front was empty, and by the looks of the undisturbed grasses, it seemed no one came often—perfect for criminal activities.

"There are a bunch of young girls and women tied up in there," Alex cautiously declared as he returned from behind the building.

"Alright then, how many of the bad guys are there?" Ivana questioned as she tied up her hair.

"Maybe twelve."

"Oh, that's many," the young woman sighed.

"Let's think of a plan first," Alex continued, his brow furrowing with concern. He ran a hand through his hair, mind racing with potential strategies. "Let's—"

Before he could complete his sentence, a deafening crash cut through the air. Ivana had already broken down the big, heavy metal doors as if they were made of cardboard. The twisted metal groaned as it fell, dust billowing up in thick clouds. She stood in the doorway before stepping into the storehouse.

"Why must you be so stubborn?" Alex yelled as he chased after her.

The inside was a mess. It was a shame they kidnapped women but still couldn't manage to keep their environment clean. Everyone within the building was stunned to see Ivana, a woman with no visible weapon or defense, surely she had a death wish.

"Who are you?" one of the men demanded, his voice sharp and challenging. He was likely the leader, his posture and tone betraying a misplaced confidence.

Ivana remained silent, her gaze methodically sweeping the room. Her eyes, cold and calculating, took note of every exit, every hidden figure, and every weapon. The tension in the room intensified as she stood there, unmoved, like a storm on the horizon.

"Hey, young lady. What the hell are you doing here?" a man tried to touch her from behind, but without a sound or any sign of struggle, the man dropped dead.

Everyone was on guard now, seeing the strange thing that had just happened.

"Hey you, what did you do?"

"You have two options," Ivana said coldly. "One, let everyone here go and turn yourselves in, or two, I beat the hell out of you and you still let the girls go."

"Wait, who do you think you are?" the man growled as they decided to take offense.

She smirked as she began to stretch her hands, deliberating cracking her knuckles. With each bend, with each crack, the guys got closer. It was nerve-racking for anyone to watch, but Ivana was nonchalant. She suddenly stopped and looked straight into Alex's eyes. "If anyone tries to escape, I won't take it lightly with you."

Alex, who was quietly watching from the entrance, scoffed, "As if any of them would survive."

The young woman they saved yesterday was amazed at how composed they were despite being outnumbered. What was even more strange was their relationship.

She sighed, her breath cold and just like that, Ivana went spontaneous. Everything around her seemed to stop in place. You couldn't see her coming. The only thing you would feel was a sharp, crushing pain as she passed by.

"They act tough, but they are just trying to hide their weakness," Ivana declared as she violently burst out of space, that's one thing about speeding up, you can't force matter to appear somewhere without energy and that burst was just matter returning to its original state. And almost every one of the bad guys dropped dead. It was terrifying, but what was more sinister were the dark veins growing around her face, pulsating her breathing now hotter.

"What...?" the guy in charge muttered.

Ivana quietly tapped his shoulder. "I don't really care what you did to them, but I will give you back the equivalence of their pain."

Before he could even try to attack, he screamed as an unimaginable amount of pain flowed through every part of his body. He struggled, but she held him tightly until he finally stopped and fell to the ground.

Alex watched in awe, recognizing the queen's unparalleled power. He couldn't help but feel a mixture of fear and admiration for her, and he was traveling with someone like her, he sighed, a mischievous smile forming around his lips. Ivana's cold demeanor hid a fierce protector.

"I hate men," Ivana scoffed.

"Does that include me?" Alex sighed as he tried to set the rest free.

"Yes."

"Ouch!"

"Mary, is that you?" a woman cried out, rushing toward the young woman with Alex. She embraced her tightly, unwilling to let her go.

"Oh, I am so sorry," Mary apologized, tears streaming down her face.

"No, don't cry. You managed to save all of us," her sister reassured her.

There is something about the way she acted towards her sister that jolted back some memories of Sera, she was the only thing Ivana considered as a family and seeing these two, it only makes clear that she needs to save Sera no matter the cost.

"Oh, sorry, these are the people who saved my life, and I asked them to help you too," Mary explained, pointing at Ivana and Alex.

The women were still scared of Ivana. Her dark veins and the display of power made her appear even more intimidating.

"Don't worry, they are good people," Mary added.

"Yes, and we're happy that we could help," Alex said, trying to ease their fear.

"Alex, we are leaving now," Ivana stated, returning to her usual mood.

"C'mon, Your Majesty," Alex unintentionally let slip.

Mary's eyes widened. The cold demeanor, nonchalant attitude, immense power, and those dark veins—it all added up.

"Queen Ivana?" Mary declared.

Everyone was stunned by the revelation. "I don't know what you're hinting at, but I am not the queen of the demon clan," Ivana replied coldly, not wanting to add to her troubles.

"Yes, you are really well informed," Alex said, smiling. "Her Majesty, the queen of the demon clan, Queen Ivana."

"Alex!" Ivana yelled.

"Wait, we were saved by the queen of the demon clan?"

"Wait, I thought everyone said she was evil."

"Alex, you're married to the demon queen? I thought she wasn't even engaged?" Mary exclaimed as it hit her.

Alex laughed. "Nope, she would deal with me if I even dared to think that. I was just getting back at her." The women were amazed by Alex's audacity towards the queen. "Even I used to think the queen was a bad person, but after working under her, I've finally seen her true light. Even though she hides it under her cold demeanor, she is nothing close to evil," Alex declared, looking towards Ivana. "Yes, she is hard and tough, but trust me, she cares..."

"Stop explaining, and let's go," Ivana sighed, preparing to leave the building.

"Your Majesty, we really appreciate your help. Thank you. We will never forget your kindness," they all collectively declared.

Ivana stopped in her tracks, their words stirring something inside, but quickly pushed it down. "Really, I don't care." And just like that, she left.

Alex sighed lightly. "Apologies, she doesn't like showing her feelings, but I know she has them... somewhere."

"Don't bother, we've heard her stories," they add. "Everyone knows about the nonchalant queen."

"Please, help her fix her reputation," Alex gestured. "All the rumors are all lies."

"After this, I will tell everyone about how we met the demon queen," they smiled.

Ivana, quietly resting on the wall outside, could hear everything and how Alex was trying his best to make them like her. He shouldn't be wasting his time. But after hearing everything, Ivana felt a sensation within her and couldn't help but smile. The day hadn't even started, but they had managed to accomplish something.

"Queen Ivana, Queen Ivana," Alex came shouting. "There you are! Let's go now."

"Call my name again, and you will join them in hell," She declared before she calmly muttered, her head lowered. "Thank you,"

"I should be thanking you. None of this would be possible without you," Alex added.

But the queen remained quiet as she started to walk away. Alex waved farewell to the young ladies they had saved.

As they walked on, Alex felt a strange sense of accomplishment and determination. Ivana's icy exterior was slowly revealing hints of warmth, and he was more determined than ever to uncover the real person beneath the iron crown.

The day pressed on as Ivana and Alex rode their horses at a breakneck pace, the wind whipping past them, the landscape disappearing into a mix of greens and browns. The beautiful scenery was lost on Alex, who couldn't stop worrying about Ivana's strange silence. Since their last encounter in the town, she hadn't been herself. It wasn't her usual cold silence; this felt more troubled.

Suddenly, Ivana pulled her horse to a stop, wincing as she reached for her back. Alex immediately noticed.

"Are you alright?" he asked, concerned in his voice.

"I'm fine," she snapped, forcing a tight smile. "Let's continue."

They got back on the road, but Alex couldn't shake the feeling that something was wrong. Her pain seemed more than physical; it was as if she was wrestling with something deeper.

Night fell, and they made camp in a dense part of the forest. The fire crackled, casting flickering shadows around them. Despite the calm, Alex's mind was buzzing. Ivana was unusually quiet, and he couldn't ignore the pain that occasionally crossed her face.

As they sat by the fire, Alex watched her struggle to reach something behind her back. She was clearly uncomfortable.

"Are you really fine, Your Majesty?" Alex asked again, softer this time.

"What is wrong with you? I said I'm fine," she retorted, her voice tinged with anger.

"No, you're not. You're hiding something," Alex insisted, standing up.

"Alex! Sit back down. I told you I'm completely fine," she yelled, her voice betraying her pain.

"If that's true, let me take a look," he said, stepping closer.

"Take a look? If you take another step, I'll kill you," she threatened, barely holding her composure.

Alex scoffed and moved closer. He felt like something cut and wrapped itself around his leg. It felt strange then suddenly, he was hit by a force that crushed his bones and made it impossible to move or breathe. A sharp crack echoed through the camp, and Alex cried out, clutching his left leg.

"Shhh," Ivana gasped, her eyes closed. She hadn't meant to hurt him, despite her threats.

"Calm down, Your Majesty. I'm fine," Alex panted, still trying to reach her. "But now I really want to know what's wrong with your back. What are you hiding?"

Unable to bear it any longer, Ivana quickly dematerialized, leaving Alex alone with his pain and confusion. "I was just trying to help," he muttered, binding his wound with strips of cloth. This was the second time she had injured him on their journey—how typical of the demon queen.

"That's going to leave a mark," Alex sighed as he splinted his leg with two straight branches. The pain was intense, but it had to be done if he ever wants it to heal quickly.

"I shouldn't have pushed her so hard," he admitted. "She needs her space. What is he even doing, is he trying to kill himself?" He stared into the fire, waiting for her return. Sleep tugged at his eyelids, and he finally lay down, drifting off despite his worry.

He woke up to the sound of footsteps. Ivana had returned, her presence quiet. She lay down across the fire from him, her eyes reflecting the flames.

"How's the leg?" she asked softly.

"It hurts, but it's not that bad," Alex replied. "I apologize for my actions. I was just trying to help, but it seems I only made it worse."

She was silent for a moment before responding, "Look, next time I tell you to stay away, please don't push me. It has never ended well for anyone who tried."

Alex chuckled, breaking the tense silence.

"What's funny?" she asked, annoyed.

"Nothing. It's just that you're really complicated, and it only makes me like you more. Weird, isn't it?"

"It's like you have a death wish."

"Relax," he said. "But really, what's wrong with you? Can I at least know a bit? I'm worried."

The camp fell silent before she sighed. "You are really annoying, you know that."

"Says the nonchalant queen."

"If you must know, I'm fine. Really, it's just a backache."

Alex wasn't convinced, but he decided not to push her further. "Alright, if you say so," he yawned, sleep overtaking him again. "Good night."

He drifted off, the night finally quiet. It had truly been a strange and exhausting day.

Later, in the middle of the night, Alex stirred, half-awake. He sensed Ivana's restlessness, her struggle with something. But interfering might provoke her anger or her powers, and he wasn't ready for another confrontation, he can't ruin is beauty sleep. As sleep reclaimed him, he hoped she would find some peace, even if she wouldn't let him help.

The morning sun filtered through the leaves, casting dappled light on the forest floor. The sky was crystal clear, and the soft rustling of leaves accompanied the gentle sound of a nearby stream. Alex struggled to stay asleep, but the bright morning light wouldn't let him.

"When I need more sleep, it never comes," Alex growled as he slowly woke up, stretching his arms in a V-shape. A sharp pain in his left leg quickly reminded him of last night's events. "Ow, did you really need to go that far?" he muttered, turning to see that Ivana had left.

"Where did she go now? Did I oversleep or something?" Alex was always the first to wake up, finding Ivana still sleeping as if she had no worries. But today was different. Something was definitely wrong.

He quickly stood up despite the pain in his leg, eager to find her. He began calling out for her, his voice echoing through the forest.

Ivana sat in the middle of the stream, the flowing water rushing past her legs. She had thrown away a silver metallic bottle in frustration. "Why is it empty? Did I use it too much?" she gasped, her anger giving way to the sharp pain in her back.

She untied her cloak, fully revealing her back. Slowly, she poured water over the burning area, shivering in pain. The water wasn't helping; it seemed to make the pain worse. "Sera, I wish you were here," she muttered, tears rolling down her cheeks.

"Your Majesty!" Alex's voice cut through the air.

"No..." she gasped, quickly trying to cover herself.

"I saw everything," Alex declared, still shaken by what he saw on her back.

"Alex, leave me alone, please!" Her voice was filled with pain.

"Stop trying to act tough. I can hear the pain in your voice," he said, stepping closer. "Look at your eyes. You've been crying and probably didn't get enough sleep."

"Alex, I'm warning you, stay away," she replied, her tone turning hostile.

"I know what's wrong with you."

"Stay away."

"It's devil's poisoning."

"Shut up."

"Do you know how I found out?" Alex asked, stepping into the stream.

"Stay away!" she yelled, trying to use her powers on him. But nothing happened, and the pain grew worse. She cried out, desperately trying to scratch the burning area.

Seeing her agony, Alex quickly grabbed her hands. She struggled, but she was too weak to free herself. "Leave me," Ivana yelled, tears streaming down her face.

"Your Majesty, I know it's painful, but don't scratch it. You'll injure yourself," Alex said, holding her hands. It was strange seeing her this vulnerable.

"What do you know about me?" she cried.

"Nothing," Alex admitted. "But Sera told me."

She stopped struggling, looking into his eyes in disbelief.

"Sera told me about the devil's poisoning and how it always affects your back. I don't know the full extent of your pain, but if it's making you cry, it must be unbearable," Alex explained.

She was speechless, unable to believe that Sera had revealed such a secret. Did Sera trust him that much?

Alex gently pulled her into an embrace. She resisted at first but then gave in, resting her head on his chest. The water flowed between them, its gentle sound calming. During the embrace, Alex caught a glimpse of her back. It was just as Sera described: a black char that slowly ate at her skin, spreading towards her spinal cord.

"Your Majesty, you are truly a strong woman," Alex said softly.

He carefully helped her out of the water and guided her to a rock near the riverbank. "Wait here. I need to get something," he said. "Please, hold on and don't scratch. I'll be back in less than a minute."

She nodded weakly. Alex rushed back to the camp, moving as quickly as his injured leg allowed. He shouldn't be running like this, but he had no choice. Pouring out the contents of his bag, he desperately searched until he found a shiny metal bottle with strange inscriptions. Grabbing it, he hurried back.

"Ah! I found it," Alex declared, panting as he approached Ivana.

She turned to see him carrying the bottle, her eyes widening in realization. It was the same bottle Sera used for the ointment.

"How did you...?"

"Oh, Sera."

"But...?"

"I'll explain after I apply this," Alex said, moving towards her back.

"Don't bother. I'll do it myself," she insisted.

"Your Majesty, Sera told me you have trouble reaching your back," he said gently.

"I'm fine. I'll manage," she declared, trying to take the bottle, but Alex held onto it firmly.

"Look at yourself. If you were fine, you could have broken my hand and taken the bottle by force. But you're struggling," he explained, slowly releasing her hands. "I know you don't like people helping you, but please, let me just help this once."

She remained silent, then slowly nodded, letting her cloak drop to her waist.

"If you look..." she began.

"Relax, I'm not like those men. I know how to control myself. Besides, why would I cause trouble for myself with a monster like you?" he joked lightly. "I don't want to die before I even start living."

"A monster? Right," she sighed.

He moved behind her, his eyes widening at the sight of the burns. They followed the path of her spine from her neck to her waist, more concentrated around her lower neck. The charred skin burned slowly.

"I'm going to rub in the ointment now," he said softly, beginning his careful task

Chapter 15

Alex carefully poured a small amount of the ointment into his hand, the strange, shimmering substance reflecting the sunlight. As he gently applied it to Ivana's back, she shivered, a mix of relief and pain washing over her. The sunlight filtered through the trees, casting dappled patterns on the ground and adding a serene backdrop to the tense moment.

"Hold still. This should help," Alex said softly, his voice steady despite the gravity of the situation. The black char on her back sizzled and hissed as the ointment made contact, slowly beginning to fade.

–"C'mom stop moving," she commanded.

Ivana bit her lip, her body tensing as the ointment worked its magic. "It burns," she whispered, her voice trembling.

"I know," Sera replied, her hands steady. "But it's the only way to draw out the poison. You'll feel better soon, I promise."–

As he worked, Alex couldn't help but marvel at her strength. Despite the immense pain, she remained composed, her eyes closed, focusing on her breathing. He couldn't imagine enduring such agony and still being able to stand, let alone lead.

After a few minutes, the black char had significantly receded, leaving behind raw, but healing skin. "That's the worst of it," Alex said, stepping back to give her some space as she slowly covered herself. "You should start feeling better soon."

Ivana remained silent for a moment, her breathing heavy. Finally, she spoke, her voice barely above a whisper. "Thank you, Alex."

He nodded, feeling a rush of relief. "You're welcome. Just rest for a bit. We'll continue when you're ready."

"I wonder what's inside this," Alex questioned as he raised the bottle to the sky, inspecting the strange inscription on it. It was a language that he had never seen or heard of.

"It's... it's...," she began slowly, clutching her hands on her lap. "Sera's blood."

His eyes widened in shock as he slowly brought down the bottle and looked at her in disbelief. "What do you mean it's her blood? But the stuff is crystal clear."

"It is. Well, it was," she began. "Human blood contains something that can counteract the devil's poisoning. Nobody wanted to sacrifice their blood for me, until Sera volunteered. Her blood is collected and distilled carefully, leaving the plasma, and it's further refined until it becomes crystal clear. The inscription on it keeps the contents from reacting with the bottle; it's some crazy magic."

"Wow, Sera's blood?" he muttered as he looked more carefully at the container. "What's this devil poisoning?"

She sighed as she turned her face to the sky before looking back at Alex. His face showed a genuine desire to understand. She could ignore him, but she couldn't ignore the fact he had helped her now. It wouldn't hurt if he knew about it, and besides, maybe Sera had already explained everything to him. But what was really going on between them?

Seeing how she struggled to speak up, he added, "Well, it's fine if you don't answer. I don't want to make you do things you don't want to. You don't owe me anything," Alex replied. "Just take care of yourself."

She shook her head. "No, I do. You deserve to know why I've been acting this way." She took a deep breath, wincing slightly but continuing. "The devil's poisoning… It's the after-effect of using my powers. It doesn't hurt when I use a small percentage of my power, but when it reaches higher levels, it begins to burn, leaving scars on my back. Most people think my abilities are all gain and no loss, but the truth is, they come at a very high cost. The more I use my powers, the more I get scared, and it really affects my mood."

Alex listened intently, the pieces of the puzzle finally falling into place. "That's why Sera told me about it," he said softly. "She wanted to make sure I could help you if it ever got this bad."

"Probably. It wasn't this bad until that massive teleportation I did at the Kingdom of the East and the battle we had back at the clan. Yesterday's rescue deal was the final blow, and I just couldn't take it anymore."

"Sera also told me that it also had to do with your mother. She said that…" he began before she suddenly yelled, her eyes widening.

"Shut up! Don't ever mention my mother in my presence again," she added, her pain evident before she slowly regretted shouting.

Alex couldn't help but feel like he had added to her pain. Maybe that's why she always hesitated to help. "Your Majesty, I am sorry. I wouldn't have pushed you this much if I had known."

She slowly stood up, holding tightly to her cloak. Looking at him, she couldn't help but smile. "You are really annoying."

"What?"

She looked at him, her eyes filled with gratitude and something else—respect. "Thank you, Alex. For everything."

He smiled, feeling a warmth spread through him. "Anytime, Your Majesty."

As the morning sun climbed higher, they sat together by the riverbank, the water flowing peacefully around them. For the first time in a long while, there was a sense of understanding between them, a bond forged in pain and healing.

After a while, Ivana stood up, feeling stronger. "We should get going," she said, her voice steadier.

Alex walked in front of her, but she couldn't help but notice that he was no longer limping. In fact, there was no scar on his left leg; it was completely healed.

"Wait, Alex, was your leg not broken?" she questioned in shock.

He laughed nervously and suddenly started to act like it was paining him again. "Yeah, and it still hurts thanks to you," he blamed playfully.

"I am sorry about that too," she replied with remorse. "And everything I did to you."

"Hey, what happened to that nonchalant queen I used to know? Where did she go? You are definitely not her," he gestured jokingly, suddenly calling out to the forest. "Your Majesty, your Majesty, where are you? Can you hear me?"

"Do you want to get beaten again?" she replied, her expression becoming cold and nonchalant once more.

"There she is! Let's go," he laughed deeply as he continued back to the camp.

But Ivana couldn't help but feel that he was hiding something about his leg. It shouldn't have healed that fast. She still watched his leg carefully as they returned to the camp.

They made their way back to the camp, where Alex quickly packed up their belongings. Ivana watched him, a new respect in her eyes. He had proven his loyalty, and for the first time, she felt she could trust someone other than Sera.

As they mounted their horses and continued their journey, the bond between them grew stronger. The road ahead was still uncertain, filled with dangers and challenges. And as they rode on, the beautiful scenery unfolding before them, there was a new sense of purpose, a shared determination to face whatever lay ahead.

Her mother? Alex's mind buzzed with thoughts as they continued their journey. Ivana's hatred for her mother intrigued him—Queen Ivana the Second, the woman who waged war against the world with an iron fist.

"We're here," Ivana muttered as the giant gates of the Kingdom of the East came into view, a stark reminder of her mission to rescue Sera. Alex remained quiet, overwhelmed at the prospect of seeing his family again. They only knew he had been working for the demon clan, a difficult truth to convince them that he was in good hands and that the demon clan wasn't as terrible as they thought.

"Alex?" Ivana called out, breaking his reverie.

"..."

"Alex!" she repeated more firmly.

"Oh! Sorry, it's just been so long, and I'm feeling a little strange and..." he began.

"Are you about to cry?" she scoffed, watching him act all moody. Sometimes she couldn't tell whether he was acting or not. In fact, the more she looked into it, Alex seemed suspicious.

"No, of course not. I'm a man."

"Yeah, right," she sighed as she continued through the gates.

Finally, they arrived at his home. It was a large house set in a vast field behind the town. Farmland? But it had different fields, not your average crops. These were rare and expensive plants, and workers were everywhere, going about their daily duties. Ivana would never have guessed he lived in a place like this; she thought he lived under some rock or something.

"Amazing, right?" Alex said as he watched her get lost in the scenery, her eyes glowing with shock or maybe surprise.

"You live here?"

"Of course, I had to live somewhere, right," he smiled as they continued into the compound. As they walked, he pointed out all the things they did here. Ivana, although impressed, still managed to keep her expression unreadable.

"And look there, it's a..." he was about to explain when a little girl called out.

"Master Alex is back!"

Everyone suddenly turned, realizing it was truly him. They all left their work to meet him, all excited about his arrival.

They were overwhelmed until a woman came out and added calmly, "Alright, alright, time to go back to work. Later we can all celebrate his arrival together, but for now, it's time to continue working."

"Yes, ma'am," they replied collectively as everyone soon disappeared the same way they suddenly arrived, without even a single complaint.

"The same way you disappeared is the same way you still arrived. Young man, do you want me to punish you?" she declared, her voice filled with authority.

Ivana was actually impressed by this display of authority. Her kind of woman. But who really is this woman, she thought to herself as she watched her carefully.

"Mother, please don't be angry. It was so sudden I didn't have enough time to tell you," he explained childishly as he hugged her. But she was all this while watching the young woman behind him. "I miss you too."

"Who's that?" she pointed at Ivana.

"Well, she is..." Before he could answer, his younger sister suddenly rushed to Ivana, standing right in front of her.

"Are you his girlfriend?" The question was so out of the blue that everyone was shocked. Ivana was actually astonished by how she just came up to her without fear.

"Do my eyes deceive me? Alex has a girlfriend?" his older sister teased from behind as she walked casually towards them. "Who would have known."

"What's wrong with you guys? You're so annoying," he replied. "She's not my girlfriend."

"Alex, you didn't answer my question," his mother declared, still looking at Ivana with a suspicious look.

"She is, well…" he started slowly, "Queen Ivana."

Almost instantly, the entire place became quiet. The sounds of birds and the wind broke the silence.

"You…" his mother replied coldly as she walked towards Ivana.

"Nice to meet…" Ivana stretched her hand for a handshake, but Alex's mother ignored it. Before she realized what was happening, a hot slap landed on her face. It was so sudden she didn't even have time to react, turning her face in the direction of the slap, still confused about what had just happened.

"You kidnapped my son," she declared at Ivana, her voice hostile. In that still moment, you could tell the hatred she had for Ivana, who had her head bowed for the first time in a while. The superior authority and power that Alex's mother displayed overwhelmed Ivana, reminding her of her own mother. Though it didn't seem like much, Ivana became afraid, a sudden response rooted in her childhood. Ivana's silence only made the moment more tense, further infuriating Alex's mother.

Seeing Ivana's pain and wanting to help, Alex quickly stepped in and pulled Ivana away, standing protectively in front of her. His mother was shocked at this but listened as he tried his best to explain.

"The queen didn't kidnap me, Mother. She saved me by taking me to the demon clan. The King wanted to kill me, and everyone cared for me in the clan. The King even attacked her clan and kidnapped Sera, her personal assistant and possibly the only person she truly cares about."

It took a while, but Alex managed to calm his mother. Realizing her mistake, she apologized to Ivana and offered to let her stay.

"Oh thanks, but I better get going," Ivana replied politely, wanting to leave, but Alex insisted she should stay. She politely refused until his younger sister begged her to stay.

"Look, she wants you to stay, so you must stay," Alex added with a smile.

Ivana hesitated, but Alex's younger sister looked up at her with wide, pleading eyes. "Please stay, Queen Ivana. We'd love to have you here."

Before Ivana could protest further, Alex's mother spoke again, her tone softer but still firm. "You're welcome to stay, Queen Ivana. I apologize for my earlier behavior. It's just... I was worried about my son."

The sudden change in the family's demeanor caught Ivana off guard. The once hostile family was now showing kindness. The two sisters rushed to her side, practically dragging her into the house. Ivana couldn't help but feel overwhelmed by their enthusiasm. It was the first time someone saw her not as the hostile, dangerous queen, but as a guest and a person worthy of hospitality.

Inside, the house was warm and inviting, filled with the smells of home-cooked food and the sounds of laughter. Ivana couldn't remember the last time she had been in such a place. The sisters continued to chatter excitedly, asking her questions and making her feel surprisingly welcome.

As they settled in, Alex's mother approached Ivana once more. "Queen Ivana, I hope you can forgive my earlier actions. I see now that you mean well, and I'm grateful for what you've done for my son."

Ivana nodded, her heart softening at the genuine apology. "Thank you. I understand your concern. I would have done the same if I were in your position."

The family's willingness to forgive and move on with anyone who had proven themselves was a testament to their strong bond. The way they were quick to forgive her and move on, still remind her of Alex, whom despite the way she treated him, he still acts as if nothing happened and even tries his best to help her — the annoyance runs in the family, she sighed.

As the evening went on, Ivana found herself laughing and talking with Alex's family, the tension from earlier melting away. Alex watched with a smile, glad to see Ivana finally able to relax and enjoy herself.

"Please, create a fireball," Alex's enthusiastic younger sister pleaded with Ivana, desperate to see her display her powers. Although Ivana could decline, she found it difficult to say no.

"Your majesty, I too would like to see it," his older sister added, displaying some curiosity. "It's not every day we get to see the famous Queen Ivana."

"Come on, let her be. She isn't feeling too well," Alex interjected as he added firewood to the fireplace. It was nearly winter in the East, and the nighttime temperature was almost unbearable.

They all looked disappointed, even their mother, who also had a peak of curiosity about the queen's mystic powers. She had heard many rumors about the new queen but wondered whether she was as powerful as the previous queen.

Alex's younger sister's disappointment was evident on her face. Ivana couldn't help but feel a bit guilty. It was strange how much this little girl was making her feel. Maybe it wouldn't be bad to display a little bit of her power.

A small glow emanated from Ivana's hands, shaping into a fire floating above her palms. The heat it emitted was pulsating and attracted everyone's attention in the room.

"Wow," Alex's younger sister exclaimed, awed by the strange sight. Everyone admired the beautiful display of fire in Ivana's hands.

"Nothing less from the queen of the demon clan," Alex's mother applauded.

Ivana smiled as the little girl became even more curious about the flame, reaching out to touch it.

"Don't…" Before Ivana could say anything, her flames suddenly turned black and disappeared into a puff of dark smoke. Suddenly, she coughed into her hands. When she looked at her hands, she was shocked and terrified.

"Your majesty?" Alex asked, concerned at her sudden display of shock.

She turned her hands towards Alex, her face still surprised. Alex too was shocked by the sight of blood on her palms. "But how?"

"Ah…!" she cried as she tried to reach her back, which was suddenly steaming, the smoke clearly visible. It was evident she was becoming uncomfortable. Trying to stand up, she stumbled, but Alex quickly caught her. "Don't worry, I'll do it myself."

Before she could take another step, she nearly fell, but he held her up. She was suddenly in a lot of pain and cried out. Everyone stood up, confused by what was happening. She grabbed Alex tightly, the intensity of her grip conveying her pain.

"Alex, what's wrong?" his mother asked, seeing Ivana in such distress.

"She isn't feeling well. Mica, please, get her room ready," he commanded his elder sister.

"Hey, don't command me," she retorted while still going off to prepare the room. After a while, she finally came back, and they both helped Ivana to the guest room.

He carefully let her sit at the edge of the bed as his sister rushed to bring back an ointment bottle.

"Wait, what's that?" his older sister inquired, eyeing the strange-looking container.

But Alex was focused on Ivana as she slowly untied the back of her dress, revealing her scarred back.

"What are you doing?" his sister added in disbelief at the scene.

"Is it bad?" Ivana spoke slowly.

Alex was quiet as he looked carefully at the new scars all over her back. It was worse than the other day. It was desperately trying to spread all over her back.

"Alex, is she alright?" his mother asked, entering the room with his younger sister.

"Don't worry, she will be," he assured them as he began to apply the ointment. The burns slowly faded. He then slowly rested her on her front on the bed while her back faced the ceiling.

As Ivana lay on the bed, the ointment working its magic on her wounds, she found herself surrounded by Alex's family. Their initial hostility had melted away, replaced by genuine concern and curiosity. Alex's younger sister walked slowly towards Ivana, her adorable face etched with worry.

"Does it hurt a lot?" Alex's younger sister asked softly, her eyes wide with concern.

Ivana managed a faint smile. "Not as much as before. I will definitely be fine."

Alex's mother, who had been watching intently, finally spoke. "I'm sorry for my earlier outburst, Queen Ivana. It's hard for a mother to see her child in pain and not lash out. But I can see now that you've been through a lot yourself."

Ivana nodded, appreciating the sincerity in her voice. "Don't apologize. I understand your concern." Deep down, she had the urge to ignore her and be nonchalant about everything, but something held her back. Maybe it was Alex, or perhaps it was the memory of Sera, her true family.

The room fell into a comfortable silence as they all absorbed this moment of connection. Ivana's eyes grew heavy, the exhaustion of the day catching up to her.

"You should rest now," Alex said gently, pulling a blanket over her. "We'll be right here if you need anything."

As Ivana drifted off to sleep, she felt a sense of security she hadn't felt in a long time. Maybe, just maybe, she had found allies in the most unlikely of places.

Chapter 16

The next morning, Ivana woke to the sound of birds chirping and the smell of breakfast cooking. She slowly sat up, her body still sore but significantly better than the night before. The room wasn't as grand as hers, but it was impressive, from the large windows through which she could see workers going about their daily duties, to the polished wood floors and furniture. The bed, fit for a queen, occupied a significant portion of the room. Alex's mother appeared in the doorway, a warm smile on her face.

"Good morning, Queen Ivana. I hope you slept well. Breakfast is ready if you're hungry."

Ivana nodded, feeling a sense of gratitude. "Thank you. I could use something to eat."

When she arrived at the dining area, everyone was seated except for Mica, Alex's elder sister, who was helping their mother bring the dishes. Watching them work happily together reminded Ivana of what she never truly had—a mother who cared. Alex's younger sister suddenly rushed over, grabbed her hands, and brought her to the dining table, prompting her to sit next to her. Ivana was always amazed by her boldness.

As she joined Alex's family at the breakfast table, she noticed the atmosphere was much more relaxed. They chatted and laughed, making her feel like a part of their family. Even Alex's younger sister, who had been so eager to see her powers, was now more respectful and kind. The warmth and hospitality they had shown her eased some of the tension she felt. She remembered all the times when she had a proper family—when she used to have one. As she ate slowly, watching how Alex constantly fought with his elder sister over who got to finish the last bit of food, she couldn't help but smile. It reminded her of how she always fought with Sera over the littlest unnecessary things. But the weight of her responsibilities suddenly settled heavily on her shoulders. She needed to save Sera. She knew she had to leave.

"I appreciate everything you've done for me, but I need to return to save my friend," Ivana said, her voice steady but firm.

Alex's family exchanged glances, a mix of concern and understanding in their eyes. Alex, however, was not ready to let her go just yet. He couldn't even continue eating; he lost his appetite as he watched the Queen, not understanding why she didn't think everything through.

"What?"

"You heard me," she replied nonchalantly, her voice cold and calm. She stood up from her seat in an attempt to leave, surprising everyone. Alex quickly rushed and gently took her arm, leading her into a quiet corridor, away from the others.

"Ivana, you're not strong enough to leave yet," he said, his tone a mix of worry and determination. "You need more time to recover."

"I've been through worse," Ivana replied stubbornly, her eyes challenging his. "I can't stay here and hide while my people need me."

"Who said you are hiding? I understand that you are concerned about Sera…"

"What do you know about me? I brought you back to your home, and what joined us is no more, so let me be."

"Look at yourself. You need to rest. I know Sera would agree too," Alex declared.

"Shut up! You don't know anything about Sera," she yelled, the pain in her voice evident, but she was still trying to appear strong. Since her mother died, she had to live with the curse of carrying her name and legacy. She tried to walk away, but the more she walked away the more it drew her back to the darkness.

Alex sighed, realizing she wasn't going to back down easily. His expression hardened with determination. "You're acting stubborn, Ivana. And if you won't listen to reason, then I'll have to make you."

Before she could react, Alex pressed her against the wall, his hands firmly but carefully holding her arms in place. Ivana's heart pounded in her chest at the sudden closeness, her breath catching in her throat. The intensity in his eyes made her feel both vulnerable and strangely captivated.

"Why are you doing this?" she whispered, her voice trembling slightly, a mix of anger and something else she couldn't quite place. "Let me go this instant." She tried to pull away from his grip, but surprisingly, she couldn't. She was using her strength, but he wouldn't even react. The force she used should have been able to rip his hands off, but he managed to still hold her in place. She found Alex strange, but this was making her lose confidence in herself. Looking into his eyes, she kept looking at her. "Why... why?" she cried, lowering her head as she admitted defeat.

"Because I care about you," Alex said, his voice softening but his grip still firm. "I can't bear to watch you like this, hurting yourself more when you're already in so much pain."

Ivana's resolve wavered as she felt the sincerity in his words and the gentle pressure of his hands. Her heart beat even faster, a mix of emotions swirling within her. She wanted to argue, to push him away and prove her strength, but the truth in his eyes disarmed her completely. Tears welled up in her eyes as the realization hit her. She had always been so strong, so unyielding, but here was someone who genuinely cared for her, someone who saw through her facade and still stood by her. Why would he even declare that he cared for her? She didn't need anyone's care.

"I don't care about anybody...".

"Ivana," Alex whispered, his voice breaking as he saw her tears. "Please, just let yourself be vulnerable for once. It's okay to need help."

A sob escaped her lips, and she collapsed into his arms, burying her face in his chest. Alex held her tightly, his own eyes glistening with unshed tears. The feel of her trembling against him, the raw vulnerability she was showing, stirred something deep within him.

"I'm here for you, even though I am not as strong as you," he murmured, his voice soothing. "I'll always be here for you."

They stood there for what felt like an eternity, wrapped in each other's arms. The world around them seemed to fade away, leaving only the two of them in their moment of shared vulnerability and connection.

Alex gently lifted her chin, his eyes locking onto hers. "You don't have to do this alone, Ivana," he said, his voice barely above a whisper. "Let me be there for you."

Ivana nodded, tears streaming down her cheeks. "Thank you, Alex," she whispered, her voice breaking. "I've never felt this way before."

Alex leaned in, his forehead resting against hers. "Neither have I," he admitted, his voice filled with emotion. "But I wouldn't trade this moment for anything."

Their lips were inches apart, the tension between them palpable. Alex hesitated for a moment, searching her eyes for any sign of hesitation. When he found none, he closed the gap, pressing his lips gently against hers. The kiss was tender, filled with all the unspoken emotions that had been building between them.

When they finally pulled apart, both were breathless, their hearts pounding in unison. Ivana rested her head on his chest, listening to the steady beat of his heart.

"You know I can have your head cut off for this," she muttered again.

Alex smiled, his arms still wrapped around her. "I know, but it was worth the risk."

"What the..?" His elder sister interjected, her mouth wide open as they quickly separated from each other. She had witnessed everything.

"...."

"Wow...," she muttered.

"What are you doing here?" he demanded.

"Mom wanted to know whether she is still leaving," she added. "Well?" Alex looked at the Queen, waiting for her response, but she just nodded and kept her face straight.

"Alright, I guess I will leave you two to continue your love thing or whatever." She turned and left, leaving Alex and Ivana in awkward silence. They couldn't even look into each other's eyes again.

"This is awkward," he declared.

"...," she turned to walk away. "This still changes nothing. You will pay for kissing me."

Chapter 17

It had been less than a week, but Ivana had been recovering quite steadily, almost to her former self. She trained a bit, though not too seriously, just to see how much of her power she could use before the devil's poisoning started setting in. Even with the training, she wasn't at her fullest, but that wasn't an issue. She just needed to get Sera and get back to the clan. However, she wasn't the kind of person to do that quietly; she would destroy the entire palace if necessary.

"Are you really leaving?" Alex's younger sister asked, her cute eyes tearing up as she looked at Ivana. Her small frame trembled slightly, her hands clutching the edges of her dress.

"I have to. I can't stay here forever," Ivana replied, rubbing the young girl's hair gently. She had grown fond of her.

"C'mon, let her be," Mica, Alex's elder sister, added as she gently pulled the young girl away from Ivana's embrace. Mica's movements were soft yet firm, revealing the quiet stare between Ivana and their mother. Mica's eyes held a mix of respect and curiosity, recognizing the strength and vulnerability in the woman before her.

"It was nice to have you around," Alex's mother said. Her voice was calm, but there was an authoritative undertone that commanded attention. She stood with a regal bearing, her posture straight and eyes steady. "Maybe, someday you could come and visit."

Ivana nodded calmly before catching sight of Alex, who quietly stared at her from a distance. He stood by the doorway, his hands shoved into his pockets, his expression a mixture of hope and resignation. She knew what he was thinking, so she walked slowly toward him, her expression nonchalant and unreadable. Her steps were deliberate, each one echoing the weight of her decisions.

She stopped at arm's length from him, staring straight into his eyes. Her gaze was intense, searching for something beneath his calm exterior. Unable to hold her gaze, he looked away, his shoulders tensing.

"I guess you are really going to leave," he said, his voice barely above a whisper.

Ivana remained silent, her eyes never leaving his face.

"Please, don't push too much and end up hurting yourself," he pointed. "And I pray you find and rescue Sera, and-"

"..."

"Is there something wrong?" he asked, his brow furrowing in concern.

Ivana stepped closer, their bodies very close. He could hardly breathe at such proximity, the scent of her mingling with his own. His heart raced, wondering what must be going through her mind.

Almost instantly, she hugged him tightly. Alex was taken by surprise, his arms instinctively wrapping around her. Everyone watched in silence as the Queen held him quietly. She slowly let him go before leaning toward his right ear.

"Did you think I would forget about what happened the other day? Everything comes with a consequence," she whispered calmly. Alex was shaken by the sudden aura she emitted; it was clear she was threatening him.

She slowly let go of him, smiling at the confused Alex. "I should be leaving," she added, releasing him completely. She walked away from the family, her steps measured and purposeful. She climbed onto her horse, her back straight and eyes forward, and rode off until she disappeared from the horizon.

"Are you going to miss her?" Mica asked as she approached her brother. She placed a hand on his shoulder, her touch both comforting and inquisitive.

"Maybe, I think, seriously I don't know," he replied, still thinking about what the Queen had said. It seemed like she wouldn't really be angry, but she was very good at hiding her real intentions. Either way, this might be the last time he would see her. "But one thing I know is I might never see her again."

"Mm," Mica murmured, her eyes thoughtful.

"Mommy, will she come back again?" Alex's younger sister asked, holding her mother's hand tightly. Her voice was small, filled with the innocent hope of a child who didn't understand the complexities of the world.

"That's not for us to decide," her mother replied, her voice gentle but firm. She lifted the young girl into her arms, the two of them disappearing back into the house together with

Mica, leaving Alex to ponder and recall everything that had transpired between him and the Queen.

From the day they met at the market to when she teleported everyone to the demon clan, to when she forced him into working for the demon clan, she was really cunning and heartless. The journey they took to get here only made it clearer; it was hard to believe that this was the same Queen who had given the impression that she would kill anything that touched her. Though it wasn't smooth sailing with her, there was progress-a lot of it-and trying to understand her had only made him grow feelings for her.

"Oh, who am I kidding," he sighed. "Once she gets better, she might just get back to being all nonchalant again."

But one thing that still stayed in Alex's mind was finding out the complete truth about why she hated her own mother to the core. All these thoughts and memories washed over his mind as he looked into the horizon, hoping that one day the Queen would finally allow herself to be happy.

Arriving outside the king's palace, Ivana wasn't completely surprised by the sheer increase in the number of watchers and soldiers patrolling the palace walls. Archers lined the battlements, their bows ready, eyes scanning for any sign of intrusion. It was as if they all knew she was coming. Even though she was almost at full power, it wouldn't be easy to get Sera silently. If she were like her mother, with just a snap of her fingers, the entire east would have been under her control, but that was someone she would never want to become.

As she surveyed the heavily guarded entrance, she sighed. "I guess I will have to change my personality."

One of Ivana's abilities was to shapeshift, though it wasn't true shapeshifting. She could cover herself with her dark energy and fine-tune it to appear like another person, even though her body remained the same.

Drawing on her powers, Ivana cloaked herself in a shroud of shadows, her form shifting and blending until she appeared as an ordinary maid. Her clothes morphed into the simple attire of a palace servant, her face unrecognizable. Taking a deep breath, she approached the gates, her steps confident yet unassuming. With her new cover, she could enter the gates more confidently.

Her gaze landed on a young guard standing near a side entrance, looking bored and somewhat distracted.

The guard looked her up and down, suspicion flickering in his eyes. "Who are you?"

"My name is Elara," she replied, using a name she had often used in her disguises. "I was sent by the steward to deliver this message directly to my master. Please, it's of utmost importance." Every word that came out of her mouth irritated her, the thought of subjecting herself to these animals was disgusting.

"I have never seen you before. Who is your master?" he questioned, still finding the young woman strange.

"Philip," she declared.

The guard burst into laughter along with his fellow guards. Philip didn't have a maid because he refused them.

Ivana watched quietly as the guards made fun of her. "I can make you lose your jobs," she threatened, but they still didn't take her seriously.

Then she brought out a silver seal with the royal initials of the Kingdom of the East. Seeing this, the guards were shocked that a lowly maid like her had such a powerful seal of this caliber. They collected it to see its authenticity, and it was the real thing.

"We apologize for our behavior," they begged.

"I don't care, just take me to meet Philip."

The guard hesitated, glancing around nervously. "Alright, follow me," he said finally, leading her through the side entrance and into the palace grounds.

As they walked through the environment, she couldn't help but feel like something was watching her. It was nerve-wracking because she really felt it, as if she could sense someone she knew, probably is Sera. She needed to focus on finding and rescuing Sera; fighting the king wasn't something she wanted to do today. Maybe another day.

As Ivana followed the guard through the palace grounds, she took in her surroundings, memorizing the layout. The grand hallways were adorned with intricate tapestries and marble statues, each a testament to the king's wealth and power. Her eyes constantly scanned for any signs of Sera or potential escape routes.

The guard led her to a courtyard where Philip, one of the king's advisors, was conversing with several other officials. Philip was known for his sharp mind and even sharper tongue, a man who rarely tolerated interruptions but who often had respect for Queen Ivana. Ivana steeled herself, adjusting her posture to appear as deferential as possible from the others.

"Philip," the guard called out, his voice respectful yet cautious, "this maid claims to have an urgent message for you, bearing the royal seal."

Philip turned, his eyes narrowing as he scrutinized Ivana. "What is this about?" he demanded.

Ivana stepped forward, keeping her head slightly bowed. "My lord, I have a message for you, but it must be delivered in private," she said, her voice steady despite the rising tension.

Philip smiled a little, then nodded. "Very well. Follow me."

Ivana followed Philip into a secluded room off the courtyard. Once the door was closed, she dropped her pretense. "I'm not here to deliver a message," she said quietly, her voice now firm and authoritative. "I need your help."

Philip watched the queen's cold demeanor and slowly smiled, "You are really stubborn."

Ivana allowed a small portion of her dark energy to flicker, revealing her true identity for a brief moment. "I am here for her," she said. "But, unfortunately, I need your assistance."

Philip stared at her. "What do you need from me?" he asked, his voice barely above a whisper. "I'm not the one having some crazy abilities here."

"Tell me where she is, and nobody gets hurt," she replied nonchalantly.

He stood quietly, contemplating something.

"What?"

"Did you really try to kill the king?" he questioned.

She sighed and walked closer to him, her aura releasing more violently with each step until she was right in front of him. She leaned into him and whispered, "If I was the one who attacked him, he wouldn't be alive right now."

Philip glanced around nervously before sighing. "I can get you close to the palace dungeon, but it won't be easy. As for Sera, she's being held in one of the dungeons beneath the palace. Only the king and a select few have access."

"Nice, let's go!" she declared, her face unreadable as she walked out of the room. Philip followed her, amazed by her. She was always different with her things, especially with that cold and calm demeanor. She hardly got angry unnecessarily. But also, if it wasn't for her, his entire family would have been kidnapped and sold into the far lands. How that happened was still a mystery.

They made their way through the winding corridors of the palace, the surroundings gradually giving way to the more austere and forbidding atmosphere of the lower levels. Torches flickered on the stone walls, casting long shadows that danced eerily as they moved. The air grew colder and damp, the scent of mildew and decay hanging heavy.

Arriving at the dungeon, they hid around a corner and observed some elite royal guards standing at the entrance. Philip whispered, "I'm telling you, this place is off-limits even to me."

Ivana watched quietly, thinking of how she could use her power to silently get in, but she risked the devil's poisoning. Every time she thought of going through that pain, it reminded her of Alex. The thought of what happened between them- the kiss-still bothered her. She couldn't believe she actually allowed that, but every fiber of her being wanted to punish him. Yet, something deep inside stopped her. The mere thought of it ached her.

"Ah! Stop..." she muttered, trying to stop thinking of Alex.

"Are you alright?" Philip asked, concerned.

"You can leave now. I will handle the rest from here."

"You sure? Please don't get caught," he added.

"I won't," she declared before looking at him, her expression ever nonchalant. "But if I am caught, I'm destroying everything until I get Sera."

"You must really love her," he added.

She ignored him, watching the guards more closely as Philip returned, leaving her with everything in her hands. He wouldn't doubt her-she had proven herself already.

Ivana took a deep breath, focusing her thoughts and energy. She observed the guards, noting their routines and any gaps in their vigilance. She needed to act swiftly and precisely. With one last glance at Philip disappearing into the shadows, she prepared herself for what was to come.

The mission was far from over, and the real challenge was just beginning.

Chapter 18

Sera, a member of the demon clan by birth, was the daughter of palace servants. Following in their footsteps, she also became a servant. Recognizing her dedicated character, Queen Ivana the Second handpicked Sera to be her daughter Ivana's personal maid. Sera was older than Ivana and took her role seriously, even though Ivana made her life a living hell at the beginning.

At first, Ivana hated her and tried to get rid of her, rejecting anything her mother gave her. Sera endured much from Ivana, to the point of considering retiring from being her personal maid. Yet, Sera was resilient and always tried her best to be Ivana's friend. She couldn't understand why, but she felt that if she didn't try to show Ivana that she saw her pain, Ivana might never see the beautiful light of the world beneath the darkness her mother was casting over her.

Sera was the only one who witnessed the molestation and hardship Ivana faced at the hands of her mother, all in the name of making her stronger. Ivana was forced to endure things no child should suffer, as her mother sought to mold her into a heartless, powerful, and nonchalant queen. Ivana couldn't resist her; she dared not. Sera would wake up in the morning to see Ivana sobbing and crying alone in her room. When she tried to ask why, Ivana's mother would say, "Let her cry those childish feelings away. No child of mine will be weak." Sera never understood what Ivana's mother was aiming for. She would see her daughter in distress but acted nonchalant, always blaming it on Ivana's weakness.

The emotional hardship Ivana endured nearly wiped out her human feelings at a young age. Despite growing up, she still had a hard time expressing her emotions. Her mother had drilled into her, "You must be strong and heartless if you ever want to rule the demon clan. Remember that you're my daughter, and no daughter of mine will be weak. Your only desire should be to make the clan the greatest, and all men must bow under your rule."

One evening, a young Ivana stormed into her quarters, her body bloody and scarred from another grueling session with her mother. She was exhausted, angry, and frustrated. Sera, who had been waiting for her, was horrified at the sight.

Sera's eyes widened as she took in Ivana's state. "Ivana, please let me help you," she said gently, moving toward her.

Ivana glared at her, her eyes filled with fury. "Stay away from me, Sera! I don't need your help!" she snapped, her voice shaking with pain and frustration.

"Ivana! Ivana!" Her mother barged into the room, clearly angry, her powers already activated. "How dare you walk away from me?"

Ivana remained silent.

"You are such a disappointment," she sighed.

"Shut up!" Ivana yelled but immediately became afraid after hearing herself say that to her mother.

"Well, well, at least you have a little bit of guts in you. Now, before I return to that training ground, I should see you there before I arrive. Do you get me?" she yelled, her voice wielding power and authority as she turned to leave the room.

"I wish you were never my mother. I wish you would die, just die," Ivana replied in frustration.

Her mother, on the other hand, didn't display any disappointment towards her daughter's reply. She just walked towards her and slapped her. The room went silent with Sera watching everything happening.

"Do you think I ever wanted a child like you? You're insignificant to me. You think I care about anything you think of me? See me as a wicked and cruel person, I will make you a weapon of power," she yelled at Ivana, who was trembling and still holding her face where she was slapped. "You will see whatever I am doing is for your good."

"My good?... I hate you," Ivana replied calmly.

"No, you will thank me," her mother replied with a smile.

Desperately wanting to retort, Ivana said, "Is that why dad left you for another woman?"

That did it. Her mother's expression changed as she smirked, her hands glowing with dark energy. She moved in again to land a punch on Ivana. Seeing that the Queen intended to harm Ivana, Sera quickly put herself in front of Ivana to protect her.

"Please, don't hurt her again, please," Sera cried desperately, tears rolling down her eyes. The queen stopped and retracted her hand, looking straight into Sera's eyes. "I might not know everything here, but please don't hurt her anymore. She can't keep up with you. You became the great Queen Ivana the Second, but you can't expect her to be like you in the blink of an eye. Please let her rest, even for today. She is really hurt."

The queen smiled at Sera before turning to look at Ivana, who was facing the floor and sobbing. She added, "Tomorrow morning, first thing, I want you in my room."

Hearing this, Ivana trembled. Every part of her body couldn't compose itself; she shook in fear, her eyes widened, her heart pounding so hard in her chest. "Her room!" Sera was disappointed she couldn't do anything helpful as she watched the queen leave the room.

"Ahhhhh!" Ivana screamed, her anger evident.

"Are you alright?" Sera asked.

"I told you I don't need your help," Ivana snapped.

Sera didn't flinch. She knew Ivana's anger was a mask for her suffering, but still, her body was already injured, and little cuts and bruises were visible. "I can't just stand by and do nothing," she replied softly, her voice steady and calm. "Let me take care of you."

"You don't understand anything!" Ivana shouted, knocking over a chair in her rage. "You don't know what it's like to be pushed to the brink every single day!"

Sera took a deep breath, trying to remain calm. "I may not understand everything you're going through, but I can see you're hurting. Let me help you, please."

Ivana stared at her, her expression a mix of anger and despair. She was on the verge of breaking down but didn't want to show it. After a moment, she slumped into a chair, too tired to resist any longer. "Fine," she muttered, her voice barely audible. "Do whatever you want."

Sera moved closer, her hands gentle as she began to clean Ivana's wounds. "I can't imagine what you might be going through with her," she said quietly. "But you don't have to go through this alone."

Ivana closed her eyes, trying to hold back her tears. "I'm slowly losing interest in everything," she admitted, her voice trembling. "I don't know how much longer I can keep doing this. I want to kill myself, but I know she will just resurrect me back."

Sera paused, her heart aching for Ivana. She wished she could do more to help, but she knew that just being there for her was important. "No matter what happens, I will always be your friend," she said softly. "I will always be here for you."

Ivana opened her eyes, looking at Sera with a mixture of gratitude and sorrow. "Thank you," she whispered, her voice barely above a whisper.

Sera continued to tend to Ivana's wounds in silence, her presence a source of quiet strength and support. In that moment, the bond between them grew stronger, forged in the crucible of shared pain and resilience.

As time went on, Ivana started to open up more to Sera. Their conversations became deeper, and Ivana began to share her deepest fears and dreams. Sera's loyalty and dedication to Ivana were unshakeable, and she became Ivana's most trusted ally in the palace.

One night, after another brutal training session with her mother, Ivana returned to her quarters, collapsing on her bed. Sera was there, waiting for her as always.

Ivana looked at Sera, her eyes hollow. "Why do you even care?" she asked, her voice barely a whisper. "Everyone else just follows orders."

Sera sat beside her, her expression gentle but determined. "Because I see the real you, Ivana. Not just the future queen, but the person behind all this pain. You deserve to be cared for."

Ivana's eyes filled with tears, but she quickly wiped them away. "I've been told by my mother to be strong and suppress my every feeling. My mother said I have to crush every desire from my heart."

Sera reached out, taking Ivana's hand in hers. "Strength doesn't mean being heartless. It means enduring and still caring despite everything. And you have a heart, Ivana. It's what makes you strong."

Ivana squeezed Sera's hand, "I am not sure I will still have a heart in the future." Trying her best to see a glimmer of hope. "Sera. Please don't allow me to turn out like her."

Sera smiled softly. "I will try my absolute best."

Their bond grew stronger with each passing year, forming the foundation of a deep and enduring friendship that would withstand the trials they were yet to face. And yet, although Ivana didn't quite turn out the same way as her mother, some of her mother's traits managed to sink and engrave themselves into her.

Sera's resilience and unwavering spirit played a crucial role in Ivana's life, helping her navigate the treacherous path of royal duties and personal growth. To Ivana, Sera was the best thing that had ever happened to her

The dungeon was shrouded in darkness, with only faint rays of light seeping through a tiny, barred window high above. Flickering torches cast sporadic glows on the cold, damp stone walls, creating eerie shadows that danced with every movement. Water dripped steadily from the ceiling, creating small puddles on the uneven floor, while the scurrying of rats echoed through the silent, oppressive air.

After a while, Ivana decided to try a little trick on them. She emerged from the corner, her body already morphed into Elara. She walked gracefully towards them, keeping her composure and expression unreadable—a straight face. They didn't move much, just watched her approach until she got really close.

"What's your business here, girl?" one of the guards barked, his eyes narrowing with suspicion.

"I am sorry to disturb you men, but His Majesty sent me to check up on the prisoner," she explained, keeping her composure strong and confident to prevent them from suspecting her.

"His Majesty doesn't allow anyone in here except himself, no matter who they are," he said sternly. "Which means you are a spy."

They immediately pointed their spears at her, ready to attack if she moved. She just smirked, trying to come up with a counter.

"Who are you?" they demanded.

"..." She remained silent.

"Speak up, or you die here," they said once more as they got closer to her.

She rolled her eyes and sighed before pulling out a necklace from underneath her clothes, which she showed to the guards, who were left surprised.

As it dangled in her hand, a seal became visible. What shocked them was its color—a golden seal with the initials of the Kingdom of the East and the royal stamp on it. There were only two of its kind: one owned by the king and the other by his late wife.

"Do you think we are fools? It's probably a fake," one of them declared. "The king would never give his seal or his wife's seal to anyone."

"Catch," she said coldly as she threw the seal towards one of them, who caught it gracefully.

While one guard remained on high alert, the other examined the seal with expert scrutiny. "Is it real?" he asked after a moment. Elite guards were specifically trained to identify authentic royal seals, recognizing crucial details such as the exact positioning of the initials, the quality of the material, and the precision of the inscriptions.

After a few tense moments of scrutiny, one guard asked, "Where did you get this? His Majesty wouldn't give his seal to just anyone."

She sighed. "Except if I was his possible future wife, right?"

They exchanged glances before one added, "Even if that was true, why haven't we, the elite guards, heard of you?"

"Maybe you did, but it escaped your mind. Not everything His Majesty wants to stay out, and if that mad Queen Ivana finds out, I will be in danger," she explained before adding, "Yes, I know it's strange for you too, but just give me five minutes to check on the prisoner, and I will go and report to His Majesty. If you still don't trust me, I can go back to His Majesty."

They exchanged glances again, hesitant at first. They didn't want to make the king mad, but the chances of her being genuine were high. Finally, they declared, "Five minutes and nothing more."

"Thank you," she smiled. "Don't worry, I promise I won't get you in trouble. I might even promote you two if I become queen."

They were grateful for the offer as they opened the pathway leading to the inner dungeons. It was dark, but the fact that they were guarding it meant there was someone or something in there. Walking into the dungeon, she looked at the empty cells on each side of the way.

"Five minutes," one guard reminded her.

"Yeah, don't worry, it will be less than that," she muttered.

Ivana moved from cell to cell, holding a torch she had taken from the wall. The emptiness of each cell puzzled her—why were the guards protecting an empty dungeon? As she progressed down the dim corridor, an unsettling silence enveloped her. Reaching the end of the dungeon without finding Sera or anyone else, she stopped, her frustration mounting in the oppressive darkness.

"Come on, where are you?" she sighed. After some minutes of searching, she began to think maybe she wasn't actually here, but still, she must be close, or why would the king be protecting an empty dungeon? She stood still in the darkness, thinking of what to do next, until she decided it was a pretty waste of time.

As she moved back, she stepped on a piece of the floor that was oddly shaped from the rest. It somehow looked like a trapdoor. She stepped on it and tapped gently, but it sounded different, which meant there should be something under it. She dropped her torch by the side and tried to use her strength to open it, but she couldn't get a grip on it. She sighed. Then she remembered something—this looked exactly like what Alex did when he was upgrading their escape routes. Although it was meant to hide secret escape routes, it had a similar design, and Alex had added a lever or something that allowed it to be opened.

She thought as she looked for anything that resembled a lever. After a while, she couldn't find anything. Using her torch to search everywhere, she still came up empty. Disappointed, she looked at the flickering light in her hands and wondered who had the time to light all of them.

"Wait..." she gasped as she turned and looked at a torch that wasn't on fire. "That's why I hate contradictions; they make you make foolish mistakes."

As she tried to pull the torch, it shifted, and background noises began to crack as the floor opened up to reveal some stairs leading down into another level. It was utterly dark, but she could hear the sobbing of someone in the darkness as she stepped down with the torch barely allowing her to see ahead.

What she saw next sent shivers down her spine and brought tears to her eyes.

Ivana stood frozen in horror, unable to utter a word as the sight of her frail, blood-drained body sank in. She stepped closer, her heart aching with each silent sob that reached her ears, until she finally sensed her presence.

It was Sera. She was strapped to a chair, attached to a device that was extracting blood from her body into a large container. As Ivana got closer, it became clearer—it was indeed Sera. Her clothes were ripped and tattered, injuries and wounds covered her body, her skin was pale and had lost its previous glow, and she had become so skinny she could barely sit up, only sobbing quietly.

Ivana couldn't mutter a word at the horror she was witnessing. She got close enough for Sera to sense someone was there.

"Please... no more... I can't take it anymore. Just kill me," Sera muttered, her voice weak and full of pain.

"Sera?" Ivana called out as she quietly rushed to set her free.

"Stop, don't hurt me," Sera pleaded, struggling against Ivana's touch as she cried.

Ivana couldn't believe it. While she was out recovering, Sera was here suffering unimaginable abuse.

"Sera, it's me, Ivana," she declared as she continued to untie her from the chair.

"Ivana?"

"Yes, it's me. Remember the stubborn Ivana," she added as she finally set her free and raised her from the chair. But Sera couldn't even stand and collapsed into Ivana's arms.

"Your Majesty," she muttered slowly. "You came for me?"

"Yes, it's me, Ivana. I am here for you, so stay with me. I will get us out of here," Ivana assured her as she looked for another way of escape but to no avail. The only way out was the same way she had entered—past those guards.

"I guess it's inevitable," she sighed as she held Sera up and made their way out of the dark place to the upper dungeon.

"But the guards…" Sera muttered weakly.

"Don't worry, I promise you will get out of here," Ivana replied quietly as she chipped off two small stones from the dungeon's wall. She placed Sera against the wall before positioning each stone on her middle fingers, each aimed at one of the guards. Almost silently, she flicked her fingers, and almost instantly, the two guards fell to the ground, the stones denting their helmets.

"Did you kill them?" Sera asked.

"No, I just knocked them unconscious," Ivana declared as she took Sera and escaped out of the dungeon.

"What is happening here?" the king yelled after seeing his guards lying on the floor.

Upon hearing his voice, the guards quickly stood up and went back to their stance. "We apologize, Your Majesty, but we didn't know what happened. It was after a young lady came with a golden seal," they explained, trying to recall.

"What?... What young lady? And which seal are you talking about?" the king demanded in confusion.

"She said that you asked her to check up on the prisoner," they declared.

"Oh no!" he muttered as he rushed into the dungeons only to find out that Sera was missing. He quickly rushed out and yelled, "That was Queen Ivana! Run, find and capture her, or I will have your entire families' heads!"

They quickly rushed out to search for them. The king pondered and sighed, "Queen Ivana."

It didn't take long, but they managed to escape the palace amidst the confusion. Even with Ivana carrying Sera on her back, the escape wasn't easy. Sera was still bleeding, and Ivana was in a tight spot, unable to use her abilities effectively.

As they dashed through the forest, Ivana's face remained nonchalant, though her mind raced with questions about why they were extracting Sera's blood. Of all the things they could do, why focus on her blood? There was no way the King found out unless someone spilled the beans. She shook her head, trying to focus. All that mattered now was getting Sera to a safe place for treatment, but where?

"Queen Ivana."

She suddenly stopped in her tracks. Ahead of her was the same dark, smoky figure that had previously attacked her when she first visited the east and again back at her clan.

"You never cease to amaze," he declared out loud. "You managed to get Sera back without me even noticing."

"What do you want?" she inquired.

"What do I want?" he said slowly, progressing towards her, each step echoing with his aura of dark energy. "I don't want anything. I am merely an enforcer of the covenant," he sighed, still progressing slowly.

She watched silently, still thinking of what to do and how to escape while avoiding a major fight. She also began to step back, trying to maintain the gap between them.

Chapter 19

"What covenant?" she asked, her eyebrows raised in confusion.

"Covenant... covenant... hmm, what was it," he muttered playfully. "Oh yes. Your grandmother, Queen Ivana the First, was desperate for power to protect the demon clan. She asked for it, and we gave her all the power she needed to rule the world. The Covenant of Nether. But in exchange, every first daughter of her lineage must continue with the covenant. A simple exchange."

"Pbbt," she blew raspberries. "Covenant my foot. Get out of my way, or else I will eliminate you from existence."

He clapped loudly, applauding joyfully, but as he got close, his clap became slow and almost sarcastic and nonchalant. "And how will you do that with the devil's poisoning?"

Her eyes widened a little, but she quickly hid her shock. How did he know that? She pondered, but at that moment she thought, based on their last fight, she didn't have the power to match him. He was on another level. She needed to find a way to escape now and fast.

"Aww, it's so cute when you think you could escape me," he sighed. "Your thirty days are up. Make your decision now: join us and stop being stubborn, or we strip you of your abilities and end you here. Your pick."

"Sera," she called calmly as she drew back even more, her eyes filled with defiance. "Hold on tight, it's about to get rough."

Before she realized what was happening, the figure appeared right in front of her, landing a knee strike straight into her stomach. The impact nearly broke her; blood spattered out of her mouth, but he still held her as he whispered, "You belong to us and you have to work under our rules or..."

Almost instantly, despite the pain, she grabbed his head and headbutted it so hard that the sound of her skull hitting his echoed through the forest. He quickly let her go, staggering back to recover from the sudden impact.

"Of course, you are relentless," he sighed as he turned back to face Ivana, whose head was bleeding. "And that's what makes you even more interesting. But look at yourself, already a mess before we even start."

She smiled sinisterly, "Yeah, you are probably right, but now I know you feel pain, which means I can defeat you."

"Ha!" he scoffed.

Almost instantaneously, Ivana unleashed a fire blast so hot and large that it scorched everything in front of her. The forest burned to ashes immediately; the green environment now scorched with dark ashes and sizzling wood.

As the smoke settled down, Ivana's eyes widened to see a figure coming out of the smoke, untouched and unharmed. One of her most powerful attacks that could destroy anything, but he managed to come out unscathed. She was really dealing with something out of her league.

"Haha!" He laughed, his laughter echoing through the forest. "Queen Ivana the Third, such a shame. I expected much better, but that was a coward's move."

Before she could reply, a powerful kick landed straight on her side. Trying to protect Sera, she managed to drift across the forest floor, but she couldn't gather herself; he was all over her, landing kicks and punches, even aiming for lethal strikes. He didn't stop, and she couldn't keep up, not with Sera on her back.

"Who do you think you are?" he yelled, landing a kick on her shoulder that caused her to kneel. "Do you think your clan would be alive without us? Everything you have achieved, your fame and respect, belongs to us. We made you all who you are."

"You are lying," she barely muttered, the pain evident in her tone.

Immediately, she landed a punch on him that not only crushed him into the ground but destroyed everything around the radius. Nothing was left, not even trees or grass, just a shattered and scattered landscape.

"Lying," he sighed, coughing as he rose from the ground. Her last attack had done some damage to him, his left arm barely moving. "Your powers are of the Nether. What we gave you, we can take away."

"Then take it away. I don't need it," she declared, preparing to attack again.

"There is no point. They don't want me to kill you, but now I think you are useless. There is no point in persuading you. Your mother was better," he added as he stood right in front of her, his fist covered with a black-toned fire.

Her mother. Why does everything in her life relate to that woman? The pain she had to endure at her hands still followed her up till now. She couldn't take this anymore. Why was she born into such a cruel manner of living? All she wanted was to live in peace with the ones she loved, but apparently, her destiny was already chosen.

He was about to land his final blow, Ivana trying to protect herself with her elbow, when suddenly the whole environment shook with an impact. The mere sound of it sent shivers down her spine. But surprisingly, she didn't feel a thing. Opening her eyes, she was utterly shocked to see another dark, smoky figure blocking his punch, this one with a skull on its face.

"What?" she muttered in shock.

"Run," the skull figure declared. Hesitant at first, she took the chance and ran the other way, away from the fight.

"Who are you?" the smoke figure declared.

"..."

"Which class are you from?" he added once more.

"Ahhaaa," the skull figure breathed slowly before he slightly tilted his head, looking at him. Without a single word, he attacked. The fight was explosive as both of them were neck and neck.

The forest erupted into chaos as the Skull figure and the smoky figure clashed. Each blow from the Skull figure was precise and strategic, aimed not just to injure but to disrupt the smoky figure's movements and anticipate his attacks. The smoky figure, however, was raw power incarnate. His strikes sent shockwaves through the air, each punch and kick devastating the surroundings.

The Skull figure darted around, using the environment to his advantage. He led the smoky figure through the trees, causing the larger being to crash into obstacles and slow down. With each attack, the Skull figure aimed for weak points, exploiting every opening with swift, calculated strikes. Despite being less powerful, his agility and intellect kept him in the fight.

"You're quick, but you can't hide forever," the smoky figure growled, his voice echoing through the forest as he swung a massive arm, barely missing the Skull figure, who ducked and countered with a sharp kick to the knee, causing the smoky figure to stumble momentarily.

The Skull figure's movements were fluid, his attacks relentless but measured. He knew he couldn't match the smoky figure's raw strength, so he focused on wearing him down, evading the more powerful strikes and landing precise blows to critical areas. He moved like a shadow, always one step ahead, using the forest to keep the smoky figure off balance.

"Is that all you've got?" the smoky figure roared, unleashing a barrage of dark energy blasts. The Skull figure weaved between the trees, narrowly avoiding the blasts, each one leaving a charred mark on the ground. He used the moments between the attacks to strike back, targeting joints and vital points with pinpoint accuracy.

The smoky figure's frustration grew as the fight dragged on. His attacks became more wild and erratic, leaving him open to more counterattacks. The Skull figure remained calm and focused, exploiting every mistake with surgical precision.

Finally, the Skull figure leaped back, landing lightly on a branch high above the ground. He looked down at the smoky figure, who was panting heavily, his dark energy flickering with exhaustion.

"I guess that should be enough time for them to run away," the Skull figure declared, his voice calm and collected.

"What? What are you talking about?" the smoky figure demanded, his eyes blazing with anger.

"Class Sigma," the Skull figure called out, his tone echoing with authority. Before the smoky figure could react, the Skull figure vanished into thin air, leaving the smoky figure alone in the devastated forest.

The smoky figure stood there, seething with rage and confusion. He could believe the fact that he was outmaneuvered by a class such as the Sigma.—Ivana ran through the forest with Sera on her back, the dark, smoky figure's laughter still echoing in her ears. The strange skull figure had bought them precious time, but she knew it wouldn't last. Branches scratched at her face and arms, and the heavy weight of Sera made each step a struggle, but she pushed on.

She needed to find a safe place for Sera to heal, somewhere far from the palace and the King's reach. Her mind raced as she thought of several possibilities, discarding each one almost as quickly as it came to her.

Her breath came in ragged gasps, her body crying out for rest, but she couldn't stop. She thought of Alex's place. He was a trusted ally, someone she could count on, but she hesitated. Bringing Sera there would put Alex in danger, and she wasn't sure if she could risk that.

Another branch whipped across her cheek, snapping her back to the present. Sera moaned softly, her body weak and bleeding. Ivana knew she couldn't afford to be indecisive. She had to make a choice, and quickly.

Alex's home was secluded and well-guarded. It was their best chance. She adjusted her grip on Sera and changed course, veering to the left and heading towards Alex's home. Her legs burned with the effort, but she forced herself to keep going, the image of Sera's pale, bloodied face driving her forward.

"Sera, you are going to be fine" Ivana whispered, her voice barely audible over the sound of her pounding footsteps. "I will make them pay."

The forest seemed endless, but finally, she saw the faint outline of Alex's home in the distance. She pushed herself harder, each step bringing them closer to safety. The trees thinned, and the familiar sight of Alex's family fortified fields came into view.

Ivana stumbled to the door, her strength nearly spent. She pounded on it with the last of her energy, praying that Alex would answer quickly.

Moments later, the door swung open, and Alex's mother stood there with her daughters. Her eyes widened in shock at the sight of them. "Ivana, what happened?"

"No time to explain," Ivana said coldly, "she needs a physician."

Alex's mother didn't hesitate. "Bring her in, quickly."

They ushered them inside, laying Sera down gently. Alex's mother called for her daughters moving swiftly to fetch supplies. Ivana was surprised that Alex's mother was getting ready to work on Sera.

"Wait, you can treat her?"

"Yes, don't worry it isn't my first time. I am the physician in the house," she explained as she stripped off Sera clothes revealing the wounds and injuries underneath it.

Ivana stood by, her face a mask of indifference, but inside, she was worried for Sera. She watched as Alex's mother and her daughters worked to save her friend. She didn't show it, but every second felt like an eternity.

As they tended to Sera, Ivana allowed herself a brief moment of relief. They had made it. Now, it was up to Alex's mother to save Sera. She stayed close, watching every move, ready to step in if needed.

After a while, Ivana noticed that Alex was nowhere to be seen. She looked everywhere but couldn't find him. She shook her head, trying her best to focus on the issue at hand: getting Sera into a stable condition.

Sera suddenly gasped and began panting for air, her body violently shaking as if she was crying. "What's wrong?" Ivana asked, seeing Sera struggling.

"Don't worry, it's just something I touched," Alex's mother said calmly as she carefully removed a thorn from Sera's face and dropped it into a metallic tray. Amazingly, Sera suddenly calmed and relaxed, breathing slowly. "See?" she added.

Seeing Sera calm and still breathing, Ivana finally relaxed. She slowly sat on the floor, exhaling and inhaling deeply. "Now that you're fine, it's time I bring an end to this once and for all," she whispered.

She thought quietly about how she could have ended this long ago if it hadn't been for that man. She sighed, looking closely at Sera. Even today, she couldn't have brought Sera back safely if it hadn't been for the strange figure with the skull. Maybe he was an ally; if so, she could find him and recruit him. But on the other hand, this could be a master plan, and they might be family or worse, from the same secret society. What troubled her the most was the covenant and her mother. She wished she could forget about her, but her mother is always everywhere in her life — the great Ivana the Second.

Suddenly, the door burst open, and Alex entered, carrying a wooden crate filled with silverware. "Hey, I've got the...," he said, standing in shock. "Wait, Sera!"

"Oh, you're finally back," his mother added as she instructed Mia to carry the crate from him. "I don't understand how the spoons and forks in this house always get lost. And don't worry about her, she's fine."

"Your majesty!" Alex muttered, barely audible, watching the queen sitting close to Sera. Although her face was unreadable, he had been with her long enough to know when she was worried.

"When do you think she will be ready to get back on her feet?" Ivana asked.

"Well, the wounds aren't fatal, though some will leave scars. She should be alright in the next three days or a week," Alex's mother declared. "But she needs to rest for the time being."

"Yes, rest," Ivana muttered to herself before leaning towards Sera, her mouth close to her ear. She whispered, "They will be gone, they will all be gone before you wake up."

With that, Ivana left the room, leaving everyone wondering what she might be thinking. The demon clan queens always had a way of leaving their mark in history, and maybe it was her time to do so.

She barged into her room, grabbed a bottle containing Sera's distilled blood, and raised it towards the window as the silver surface glimmered in the sunlight. She sighed, thinking of what she was about to do. It was one thing to fight in a war with allies and another to fight against one of those allies. It would be bad for their reputation, but she didn't care what the world thought. If she had to burn the world to protect Sera, so be it.

"Sera, sorry, but I have to do it," she said, holding the container tightly and gulping down every last bit of the substance.

Immediately, her eyes turned black, and her veins darkened but then returned to normal. She dropped the bottle and looked out at the horizon through the window, knowing that what she was about to do might not end well for her. But now, there was no going back. Her body surged with energy, and she could feel every cell trying to split.

She sighed deeply, her mind made up. Gathering her power, she felt the energy course through her veins, building and intensifying. The air around her began to crackle with electricity, and the room darkened as her power reached its peak.

Ivana took one last look at the horizon, her face set in determination. She closed her eyes, focusing all her energy on the teleportation. The ground beneath her feet trembled, and the walls of the house shook violently. The air around her swirled into a vortex, pulling at the objects in the room.

With a blinding flash of light, Ivana's body dissolved into a cloud of dark energy. The force of her departure caused a shockwave that rattled the entire building, sending a powerful gust of wind through the rooms. Windows shattered, and furniture toppled over as the energy rippled outward.

In an instant, she was gone, leaving behind a room filled with the remnants of her immense power. The house slowly settled, the echoes of her teleportation fading away. Those left inside could only wonder at the sheer force they had witnessed.

Chapter 20

The clouds darkened as thunder rumbled, and the entire palace shook under the pressure of something coming. It was evident the aura was intimidating. Suddenly, a force dropped at the center of the courtyard, turning the entire floor into a crater. The shockwave vibrated the entire surrounding.

"What was that?" The king and his entourage rushed out to the scene. It was horrific to see the entire environment change so suddenly.

As the dust settled, there she was, standing amidst the rubble. Her eyes were hollow, revealing no emotion. Her gaze was fixed on the king, the entire environment blurred with only the king in focus.

"Queen Ivana!" the king yelled. "Do you seek death?"

She was silent as she shifted her view towards the palace, a massive and exquisite building, its structure magnificent—the pride of the east. She smiled sinisterly.

"I think it's time I show you your place amongst the rulers of this world," he declared, summoning his weapon. It materialized from the air, with only the outline at first, then slowly turned metallic and shining. The sword glittered as it expanded, an aura emanating each time a gem was added, until the inscription appeared completely and the full power of the sword was unleashed.

Without hesitation, she appeared directly in front of him, attempting to land a killer blow. But he struck her with the sword, sending her crashing across the floor. She couldn't believe what had just happened; he was never that powerful before.

"Surprised?" he smiled as he approached her.

She went for the attack again, appearing behind him, trying to land a punch, but he dodged her. She tried again immediately, but he escaped, and again and again. Until he hit her again with the sword, which she managed to block with her hands, but she sustained a cut.

She drew back, watching him closely, especially his sword, which she now discovered was emitting a hint of dark energy. It was shocking to see that he possessed such powers—unless it was that smoky figure doings. She needed to finish this quickly before he appeared. She dusted her face off, her original smile gone, her look now unreadable and cold.

"What's wrong, Queen Ivana? Have I already outmatched you?" the king mocked.

She raised her hand, displaying two fingers.

The king stared in confusion, thinking it might be some black magic.

"Two minutes. In two minutes, I will make this palace disappear, and you from history."

He scoffed. "You must be bluffing."

Her skin dried up, the veins on her face and neck darkened, revealing intricate details, but her eyes remained normal. She went straight at him again. This time, when she landed a head-on punch, the king immediately blocked it with his sword, which absorbed all the energy of the attack. She immediately teleported back to her original position.

"You can't defeat me, Ivana," he declared, readying his stance to fight back. "No matter how hard you try, I am powerful now."

She remained silent and attacked again in the same way, straight for a punch. He just blocked it, and she bounced back.

"Haven't you tried that?"

Ignoring him, she attacked in the same manner without changing any detail. This time, when she landed the punch, although he managed to block it, he still stepped back just a little. That gave Ivana a bit of confidence.

She smiled sinisterly, her grin sharp and fierce. She caught her breath, and what happened next occurred spontaneously. She did the same attack but didn't stop, increasing her speed and momentum, returning back to her original position. She continued until all you could see was dust particles going from left to right.

The ground between them eroded under her movement. The king's sword was still absorbing the energy, but the amount she was hitting him with exceeded what the sword could take. The remaining energy went straight to the king.

Before he could recover from the sudden attack, she appeared directly behind him, landing a punch so powerful that the king went crashing through the ground. Before he could stand, she was already on him, attacking. When he tried to smite her, she teleported and attacked from a random side. The attacks were worse now; the king couldn't take it anymore. He dropped to the ground.

She punched him so hard that he didn't have any energy left to fight. Then she let him go and teleported to the highest point on the palace.

"Wait, Ivana, don't," the king yelled."Don't worry I am bluffing," she smiled sinisterly and muttered some barely audible words. Suddenly, the sky formed a vortex, rumbling with thunder, and lightning appeared. Almost instantly, a massive bolt of lightning, perhaps one of the greatest in history, fell from the heavens, consuming the entire palace and reducing it to nothing. It happened so quickly and suddenly that even those present couldn't believe what they witnessed but could fear at her true power, what she was, nobody truly knows.

Immediately she was in front of him, who still couldn't believe what he had witnessed. He had never seen her powers to this extent, even in the war.

"But how?"

She grabbed his clothes, raising him to her eye level. "Because I am Queen Ivana the Third."

Seeing this, the king couldn't accept defeat just yet. He had one trick up his sleeve. He muttered some words, probably an incantation. His eyes turned black, and his veins darkened, just like Ivana's. His aura increased to a complete pure dark energy; he was a totally different person. She looked in surprise but still held him tightly. She watched as the aura ate its way from his body through her hands.

"What is this?"

"The covenant," he declared as he emitted dark energy, trying to overwhelm Ivana.

"What are you doing?"

"What?" He looked in confusion, seeing the queen unaffected. "How? But it was supposed to make it easier to defeat you."

She smiled, finally understanding what he was trying to do. "Hmm, you think that is something? Let me show you true dark energy."

Immediately, Ivana unleashed her aura. It was so powerful that you could hear the sound of it emitting from her body. It overwhelmed him, causing his eyes and ears to bleed. He was barely trying to stay conscious.

"Such a shame," she declared as she went for the kill.

Before she could strike, a force pushed her, sending her sliding across the floor. Looking to see what happened, her expression changed. There it stood, the smoke entity.

"Wow, that was intense. You almost killed him," he said, grabbing the king.

She assessed the situation. She didn't know the full extent of his power, so it would be best not to attack for now and plus her back is starting to itch. But she didn't want the king to survive after what he had done to Sera. Yet, she had to leave or else she wouldn't like the outcome.

"Look, he's in my hands. Come get him," the entity declared. Seeing the queen was reluctant, he taunted, "Don't tell me the great Queen Ivana the Third has given up."

She smiled, standing still. "Not today, but one day."

And immediately, she dematerialized from the environment, leaving no trace.

He chuckled as he dropped the king and muttered, "Unfortunately, there will not be another day." He slowly dematerialized from the place too.

She materialized, panting as exhaustion set in. "What...?" she gasped in shock, finding herself atop a mountain, far from where she intended to appear. She had never missed a teleportation point before, especially not to a familiar location. Could there be interference? Her eyes widened in realization as she sensed a higher magnitude of dark energy approaching her location—could it be him?

"And here we find ourselves again," a voice muttered as the smoke entity materialized from thick black smoke into a more distinguishable figure. Each step he took was more intimidating.

"Haaa," she gasped, slowly drawing back.

"Why did you step back?"

It was one thing to be strong, but another to be powerful. When facing someone of greater caliber, retreat could be a wise choice, as the energy levels difference in such battles could become immense, something some called "god mode". Still, the smoke entity was a formidable opponent. From their brief encounters, she knew his attacks were layered with multiple levels of dark energy, even his physical strikes.

"Hey, Ivana? What's wrong? Why are you overthinking? I thought you had the reputation of attacking first," he remarked, his tone almost sounding concerned.

"Well, that's not the case with you. You're strong," she replied, her tone calm.

"Wow, is that a compliment from the bitter Ivana?" he said, mockingly applauding, his energy multiplying with each clap. "But unfortunately, you're too stubborn, and it's been decided that you have to be killed."

She smiled faintly as she began tying up her hair. "Well then, there's no escaping you. Which means I have to defeat you."

"Let the strongest win," he declared, his aura skyrocketing.

"Show off," she smirked.

"I could say the same," he added, watching as her eyes turned completely black, her veins darkened, and raw energy emitted from her skin.

Before he could make a move, Ivana launched into a relentless barrage of strikes. She imbued her physical attacks with her energy, amplifying their effects. Her movements were swift and precise, each blow carrying a force that shook the ground beneath them. She didn't give him a moment to breathe or anticipate her attacks.

As Ivana pressed her assault, it seemed she was gaining the upper hand. The smoke entity was forced on the defensive, unable to match her relentless pace. Her blows landed with increasing intensity, pushing him back with each hit. His energy levels visibly dropped, giving Ivana hope that she could win if she kept up the pressure.

But then, a sudden, intense itch began to spread across Ivana's back, quickly escalating into a burning sensation. Her movements faltered, her speed and strength waning. Her eyes widened in realization—she knew this sensation. Was it because of the energy she expended destroying the palace?

"Such a shame," the smoke figure remarked, noticing her reduced speed and hesitation. "It's a simple side effect if you refuse the covenant—a way to help us control the strays like you."

As the pain intensified, Ivana's attacks lost their power, and the smoke entity seized the opportunity to turn the tables. He unleashed a flurry of dark energy attacks, each one hitting harder than the last. Ivana struggled to defend herself, but her movements were sluggish, and the burning sensation on her back continued to sap her strength.

Despite her injuries, Ivana fought back with every ounce of willpower she had left. She parried and blocked, refusing to yield even as the smoke entity's onslaught pushed her to her limits. Her vision blurred, and her body felt heavy, but she stood her ground.

"Wow, you are amazing, still able to fight," he said, amazed at the battered queen. "You really are an Ivana."

Finally, the smoke entity delivered a powerful blow that sent her crashing to her knees. Gasping for breath, Ivana looked up to see him hovering above her. He pointed his finger at her, and a small vortex formed, compressing his dark energy into a large orb. She smiled at the sight of the energy he was about to unleash on her.

The smoke entity's face was expressionless, his voice cold. "I wish we could have been friends, Ivana. You are strong, really strong, but not submissive."

She scoffed slightly trying to hold back the pain.

He released the energy orb, which hurtled towards Ivana with a sense of finality. It seemed all hope was lost; there was no way she could escape this attack. Even if she could counter it she doesn't have enough energy and he is too strong even in her prime she might not be able to defeat him and this large orb is just pure dark energy, where will she even put it if even she has the chance....

Her eyes widened and suddenly covered by a nonchalant expression, Ivana did something unexpected—she opened her mouth, a technique she had sworn never to use again. The orb was absorbed into her mouth, disappearing as she closed it. Her eyes and skin glowed and almost cracked under the sheer amount of improper energy she had just taken in.

"Amazing, the forbidden absorption technique of the demon clan," the smoke figure replied, astonished but not entirely surprised. "Unfortunately for you, you may not survive using it. Especially after absorbing an energy orb three times your own capacity."

The absorption technique was among the highest tier of techniques in the demon clan, allowing the user to absorb any form of external energy through their mouth. However, it came with a dangerous consequences: absorbing an energy level nine percent higher than one's own could result in instant death or worse—explosion or burning up.

"What makes you sure I will die?" she responded, her body trembling as it struggled to contain the vast amount of energy.

"Hm? Look at yourself. What makes you think you have the upper hand here? The absorption technique is just another death wish," he said, still amazed by her audacity.

"Yes, everyone thinks it's a deathwish, and it's true, but anything can happen," she smiled sinisterly before facing him directly. "But I hate contradictions."

"What?"

Before he could react, Ivana unleashed a devastating blast of energy far greater than what she had absorbed. The blast raged straight at him, burning him and everything in its path. The smoke entity screamed in pain, his shouts echoing through the entire mountain. Not only had she absorbed the energy, but she had also amplified it to an even greater level.

As the blast subsided, her mouth smoked, and she was exhausted, barely able to keep her eyes open. She fell to the ground, panting and in pain, but it felt worth it, especially since the smoke entity should have been dead by now. Her mind began to relax until a sudden burst of dark energy emerged from the fires.

"No, no," she muttered in disbelief.

"That was close. A little more, and I would have gone to hell," he declared as he emerged from the smoke, his body slowly reforming. "Ivana the Third, you're the first in history to injure me this badly. I applaud you."

She tried to stand but couldn't; her body was stiff, completely drained of energy. It seemed she might have lost for real now. The figure stepped closer to her and added, "Out of respect for you, I will end this quickly and painlessly."

As he approached her, Ivana closed her eyes, bracing for whatever would happen next. Memories flashed before her eyes—Sera and her clan, Alex and his family, and even her mother, whom she despised the most. Suddenly, a sharp noise sounded from afar, growing louder and more irritating, until it crashed right in front of Ivana.

"It's you again."

"Yeah, me."

"Why are you here?"

"I have come to save her."

Ivana opened her eyes and realized it was the same entity that had saved her when she tried to escape with Sera.

"Wait?" Ivana gasped as it turned its face, revealing a familiar skull face.

"I will protect you this time," he declared.

"I don't need your help or protection," she replied her arrogance still present even though she already down.

"Well, unfortunately for you I will help you whether you don't need me or not. But first, I need to finish this."

"What makes you think you can defeat me again, Sigma?"

"Sigma? Hmm? I don't know, honestly. I wish I could avoid this, but I always find myself in trouble."

"Ah! Yes, Ivana. I brought you a gift," he said as he produced something and showed it to Ivana. Her eyes widened in horror and surprise as he threw it in front of the smoke entity. It rolled up to his feet, and he grimaced upon realizing it was the head of the King of the East.

"Well, there are many who can replace him," he declared.

"But not many can replace you, right?" the skull figure added, readying his stance for an offensive.

"Don't defy the laws of the classes, or do you think a Sigma like you could ever defeat a Gamma class?"

"Hmm? If I was Beta you won't be talking like that," the skull figure declared as he moved closer to the smoke figure, "but it will be nice having a gamma on my resumé."

Chapter 21

The room was shrouded in impenetrable darkness, a sanctuary concealed from prying eyes. This was a place where only the master dwelled, rarely seen and even more rarely heard. The space was stark, almost barren, save for the oppressive weight of a dark, unseen force. The air itself seemed to hum with an unsettling energy, and every step he took reverberated ominously through the room, amplifying the palpable sense of dread that hung heavy in the air.

A lone figure, suffused with the purest and darkest form of energy, stood in the center, the only other presence in this sinister chamber. The echo of his footsteps grew louder as he advanced toward this entity, each step a portent of the chilling power that accompanied him.

"Have you killed the queen?" a voice rasped from behind a shadowy silhouette. The figure's presence was cloaked in an aura so powerful and malevolent that it seemed to constrict the very space around it. The room itself seemed to shrink beneath the oppressive weight of his aura, a force so formidable that even the bravest would quake in its presence.

"Not yet," the smoke figure responded, only to be met with an immediate and crushing force that slammed him to the ground.

"There was interference by another stray," he managed to choke out, the pressure intensifying with each word, threatening to crush him further. The very ground beneath him buckled under the immense force, a testament to the sheer magnitude of the master's power. If he were not a Class Gamma, he would have been obliterated.

"It was another man that belongs to us," the smoke figure added.

"..."

"A Class Sigma!" His declaration elicited a slight reduction in the crushing force, a sign that he had piqued his master's interest.

"Describe him," the silhouette demanded, his voice penetrating and deeply resonant.

The smoke figure trembled slightly, his voice barely a whisper as he described, "His major feature is his skull. It is exposed, while the rest of his body is shrouded in dark particles, much like my own."

The room fell into a heavy silence as the force receded, leaving only the eerie stillness and the pounding of hearts in the oppressive quiet.

"I was exhausted before I could finish him off," the smoke entity added, slowly rising from the ground.

"You won't be able to defeat him."

"Why...? He is just a measly Sigma," the smoke figure protested, confusion evident in his voice.

"That 'measly Sigma' is responsible for the deaths of a Beta class member," the master's voice was cold, laden with an unspoken weight.

The smoke figure's eyes widened in realization. "That was him? But maybe the Beta was weak. He was the lowest in the Class. I am the strongest in the Gamma class. I can easily defeat him."

"I am sending someone else," the master declared, his tone final and commanding.

"Why send someone else? Send me. I am stronger," he argued. "What's so special about this particular Sigma?"

Silence fell once more, thick and suffocating. "The Sigma is indeed weak, but his technique is what makes him dangerous. The stronger you are, the more formidable his technique becomes. It's crucial to send someone with a specialization in weapons and projectiles. Focus on Ivana and leave the Sigma to me."

"But..." The smoke figure began, only to be cut off by an invisible slash of energy, a clear warning to cease any further argument.

"Understood."

He turned to leave, the gravity of his master's directive weighing heavily on him. As he walked away, he pondered why his master was so adamant about not confronting the Sigma himself. He dismissed the Sigma's technique as improbable, convinced that even though he could not match the Sigma's speed and teleportation, his own abilities should have sufficed.

"You really have a stubborn son," the master murmured softly, the words dripping with an ominous foreboding.

The transformation of the mountain was swift and brutal. What had once been a lush, green, rocky surface was now scorched and ravaged, turned into a hellish expanse of burnt terrain. The skies roared with the energy exchanges between the two entities, their clashes unleashing waves of devastation that defied imagination. Amidst the chaos, Ivana watched in silent awe, unable to move, shielded by an unexpected ally whose true intentions remained unclear.

The Skull Man struggled against the smoke entity, the disparity in their strengths clearly obvious. Ivana, aware of the Skull Man's superior power compared to herself, was intrigued by the Skull Man's relentless defiance. Despite the Skull Man's undeniable strength, he was clearly outmatched. This realization fueled Ivana's curiosity about him.

The Skull Man crashed into the ground, barely able to endure the deafening force of the smoke entity's attacks. He lay there, gasping heavily, his body enveloped in the smoky aftermath of the relentless battle.

"Exhausted already?" the smoke entity taunted, floating effortlessly in the air. "I heard you were supposed to be powerful. And I also heard you were meant to assassinate her, but instead, you betrayed your Beta class partner. Now you're reduced to protecting her. It seems your fight has faltered."

The Skull Man managed a faint, defiant smile. "Well, you are actually strong."

"Ha," the smoke entity scoffed, sending a massive energy blast that hurled the Skull Man across the shattered mountain floor once more. "I don't know what he sees in you that he wants to send a Beta class after you."

"Maybe he thinks I'm stronger than you," the Skull Man mocked, his voice betraying the pain he was in.

"Stronger?" The smoke entity's eyes narrowed as he advanced with lethal intent. He unleashed a barrage of attacks, focusing on the Skull Man's face, determined to break through his defenses. He landed a solid punch, then grabbed the Skull Man's face, lifting him up for the final blow. The Skull Man, once a figure of confidence, was now nearly lifeless and at the mercy of his adversary. The turn of events was a stark reminder of how quickly fortunes could change.

"Hey, smokey."

The smoke entity turned to see a massive energy orb surging toward him, pulsating with overwhelming power. Reacting quickly, he dropped the Skull Man and tried to intercept the orb with his hand, only to find that its intensity increased, forcing him to use both hands to block it. The orb's pressure forced him back, his feet slipping on the ground, and his hands beginning to burn under its relentless force. Struggling to redirect it, he sent the orb soaring into the sky, where it exploded with a thunderous bang that echoed across the mountain.

The smoke entity stared at his singed, aching hands, then raised his gaze to find Ivana, a grim smile on her face.

"I thought you were...?"

"Contradictions, right?" Ivana smiled wider. "I took some time to regain my energy and use it with your technique. It was easier than I thought."

"It doesn't matter if you learned my technique. You can't defeat me, even if you triple your power," the smoke entity declared, advancing menacingly toward Ivana.

Ivana's smile remained. The Skull Man, with renewed resolve, leaped onto the smoke entity, wrapping his legs around the entity's thighs and his arms around his head, holding on tightly.

"Who said anything about defeating you?" Ivana declared.

The Skull Man whispered, "Reserve-amplification."

The smoke entity screamed in agony as his own energy began to violently radiate outward, tearing through every atom and rapidly depleting his power. The scene was almost surreal—witnessing the very essence of power being drained while still wreaking havoc. The Skull Man held on firmly until the smoke entity's movements ceased. When the Skull Man finally released his grip, Ivana watched in astonishment as the smoke entity disintegrated into dust, carried away by a gentle breeze.

"What?"

"Nasty stuff," the Skull Man sighed, observing the remnants of the once-powerful entity scatter into the wind.

"You should be fine now," he said, turning to face the queen. He wasn't expecting the intense focus in her eyes, nor the sudden surge in her aura.

"Who are you?"

"I'm guessing you're fine. I need to go," he replied, turning to leave. But Ivana teleported in front of him, blocking his path. "Come on, I'm not your enemy. There's no need to ask. If you piss me off, I might harm you, just like I did to him."

Ivana remained indifferent. "You can't harm me."

"What makes you so sure?"

"You're weak."

"I don't have time for this," he said, beginning to walk away. But Ivana kicked him in the side, sending him crashing to the ground.

"How dare you?" he shouted.

"Like I said, you're weak," she replied coolly.

With a resigned sigh, he grabbed her neck, squeezing tightly as he stared into her hollow eyes. "You really live up to your reputation."

Ivana gasped and retaliated with a swift kick to the side of his head. It was so fast and forceful that he couldn't react in time. The pain set in as he found himself on the floor, clutching his face.

He looked up in disbelief at the queen, who was approaching him with an unreadable expression. "Is that how you treat someone who just saved you? How did you even kick that high?"

"Answer me, who are you?" she demanded, her veins darkening as her seriousness intensified.

"Your majesty, what does knowing who I am add to your situation?" he replied, trying to back away and summon his remaining energy to teleport. "I don't have time for this. I'm leaving."

He attempted to teleport but found himself unable to. Something was blocking him. He glanced at Ivana, astonished. How could she do this? It shouldn't be possible, but she did.

"Alright, I guess we're doing this," he declared, his aura flaring as he prepared to defend himself against the advancing queen.

Before he could fully power up, Ivana landed another punch to his face. He was hurled across the floor, demolishing everything in his path. Before he could recover, she struck again, targeting his bony face with a series of fierce and precise punches. Each blow aimed to break through his mask. Her relentless assault caused a crack to spread across his skull.

"Wait, wait," he pleaded, raising a hand in a gesture of surrender. "Aren't you afraid I'll kill you with my technique?"

Ivana scoffed. "You had many opportunities to use it, but you didn't. And I think I know why."

"What do you mean?" he asked.

"Because..." Ivana began slowly, but a sudden force field pushed him back. His dark energy was compressed, reducing the amount he could use. His skull began to heal as the dark particles around him dissipated, revealing his face. "Because I know you, Alex," she said, her words heavy with meaning.

"How did you...?"

"That first day we met-was it on purpose?" she demanded, her voice fierce.

"Why the strange question? Of course, it wasn't on purpose," he replied, struggling to maintain eye contact.

"Lie to me again, and I'll kill you," she warned, a sharp cut appearing on his face, causing it to bleed. "Tell me!"

Unable to speak, he bowed his head, his gesture a silent admission of the truth.

"Why?"

"..."

"I said, why?"

"I really didn't mean for any of this to happen," he muttered.

"So it was all planned? Everything? Our first meeting, me bringing you to the demon clan? Did you know about Sera?"

He remained silent, staring at Ivana, wishing she would stop asking this questions. "Your majesty..."

"Did you know?" she yelled, her voice echoing through the mountain.

He hesitated, but if he didn't answer, she would kill him. His neck resisted, but he finally nodded.

They stared at each other in silence, Ivana's expression shifting from unreadable to silently enraged. The realization that he had been hiding something from her all along seemed to ignite a fierce anger within her. Without another word, she turned her back and began to leave.

"Wait... your majesty," he muttered weakly.

Chapter 22

"Your majesty," Lisa rushed toward the queen, who was weary but still tried to maintain a confident facade.

"Lisa."

Lisa's eyes sparkled as she grabbed the queen's hands, her joy palpable. "Sera's awake!" she declared, pulling Ivana along. Ivana followed, too drained to resist the enthusiastic child. Her mind was still grappling with the recent events. Despite their victory, she felt a gnawing sense of betrayal and anger.

They moved down the corridor, and as they approached the door, Lisa let go and darted inside. Ivana hesitated, feeling a mix of anticipation and dread. She slowly turned the handle and pushed the door open. Inside, Sera was on the bed, playing with Lisa, who was proudly displaying her toys.

"Your majesty...?" Sera's voice was soft as she noticed Ivana standing in the doorway. She could see the strain etched on the queen's face, knowing that Ivana had endured much.

Lisa hopped off Sera's lap and ran to Ivana, who approached Sera with heavy steps, trying to mask her pain from the devil's poison. As she neared, the familiar face of Sera—the one person who truly understood her—brought a sliver of comfort.

Ivana stood before Sera, who was forcing a nonchalant expression despite her concern. Sera reached out and took Ivana's hands. "Your majesty, what's wrong? You don't seem happy. I can see it in your face."

"I'm fine," Ivana replied, though her voice betrayed her.

Sera's eyes softened as she pulled Ivana into an embrace. Ivana didn't resist, sinking into the hug as Sera's arms enveloped her. "So tell me, are you really fine?"

"I am... fine."

They held each other in silence for a moment before Ivana spoke again. "What would you do if you found out you were tricked?"

"Tricked?"

"Yes, what if someone infiltrated your life only for you to discover it was all a scheme?" Ivana's voice was tinged with confusion and sadness.

Sera's expression shifted to one of genuine curiosity. "Well... if the person intended harm, then they should be cut off immediately. But if it was all part of a plan for your benefit, perhaps they were trying to protect you by hiding the truth."

Ivana sighed deeply. "What if they planned to kill you from the start, but..."

"But what?"

"They didn't."

"Maybe they had a change of heart," Sera suggested. "Perhaps they saw you weren't the enemy and realized they were mistaken. After all, the world still views us as villains. Maybe they were influenced to see us that way."

"But still, they lied to us. They knew everything," Ivana said, her frustration evident.

"So what are you planning on doing?" Sera asked.

"I want to burn him," she sighed, frustration evident in her voice. "... i just don't know what to do."

Sera raised an eyebrow, sensing that Ivana was talking about someone specific. "Wait, who is this person you're talking about?"

The door creaked open as Alex stepped into the room, taken aback by the sight of Ivana clinging to Sera.

"Alex, you're finally back!" Sera exclaimed, her eyes lighting up. But Ivana's reaction was colder. She abruptly released Sera and approached Alex with a mixture of anger and frustration. She looked straight into his eyes. Her eyes were cold and nonchalant but deep inside it feels like she could burn him right there before turning and walking straight out the door, not uttering a word. Alex sighed, feeling the weight of her unspoken resentment.

Seeing the charged moment between them, Sera began to piece together what Ivana had been hinting at—it was clear that Alex was at the center of the conflict.

"Alex, how was she while I was gone? I hope she wasn't too much trouble," Sera asked, trying to diffuse the tension that Ivana had left behind.

"She wasn't too much trouble, but I'm afraid I might have caused some," Alex replied quietly.

Sera's eyes softened as she looked at him. "I think I have an idea of what you did, but to be honest, I still trust you. I don't know why, but I do. And don't worry about Ivana. She might be angry now, but she'll get over it. She always does."

Alex felt a flicker of hope at her words. He hadn't intended for things to go this way or to drag Sera into it, but his actions were driven by a desire for revenge against the Classes that had wronged him and his mother. He felt a pang of guilt, knowing that he hadn't been honest with Ivana. His emotions were getting the better of him.

"I don't even know what to say to her. I don't think she'll ever forgive me...," he confessed, stopping half way before noticing Sera". "what..?"

Sera's lips twitched into a barely concealed smile. "Oh, nothing. It's just funny how you're worried about what to do, and she's worried about what to do. You're both just confused."

Alex remained silent.

"Let me give you a bit of advice. Ivana has never let someone who broke her trust or hurt her live as long as you have. She usually ends things instantly."

Alex's eyes widened in shock. "So, I would have been dead?"

"Yes," Sera confirmed.

"But?"

Sera sighed, "Do you want me to spell it out for you?"

They exchanged silent glances at each other. Alex looked at her expectantly, though she struggled to contain a laugh. "Seriously?"

"She likes you.:

"Seriously...?"

"Yes, seriously," Sera said, her tone softening. "It's clear she has feelings for you."

Alex's eyes widened, and he fell silent, processing her words. "Seriously?"

"Don't ask me. Go find out for yourself," Sera said with a teasing smile.

"You know she'll never admit it to me," Alex replied.

"Of course. It's nearly impossible, but not entirely. Consider it my way of punishing you for whatever you did that made her so upset. Now, if you don't mind, I need my rest. Lisa has been bouncing off the walls all day," Sera said as she snuggled into the bed.

Alex nodded and left the room, his mind racing with the revelations and the challenge ahead.

Alex stepped into the dimly lit corridor, his mind racing with Sera's words. Each step felt heavy, as if he were dragging the weight of his own guilt along with him. He reached Ivana's door, his heart pounding. Hesitating for a moment, he finally pushed it open.

Inside, Ivana was seated by the window, her silhouette framed against the twilight. The way she sat, so still and yet brimming with unspoken turmoil, made Alex's heart ache. Her posture was rigid, her eyes locked on the horizon, a mask of frustration and sadness.

"Your majesty," Alex called softly, stepping into the room.

Ivana's head snapped around. The intensity of her gaze was like a physical force, almost palpable. Her eyes, previously so firm and unyielding, were now a storm of emotions—anger, betrayal, and pain. She rose slowly, her demeanor a carefully maintained façade of icy detachment. "What do you want, Alex?"

"I wanted to talk," he said, taking a tentative step closer. "About what happened, and... what Sera told me."

Ivana's eyes narrowed, her entire posture bristling with tension. "Sera told you what?"

"Yes," Alex admitted. "She mentioned that you might still care, despite everything."

Ivana's scoff was a sharp, dismissive sound. She turned away for a moment, then faced him again with a scowl. "What Sera told you doesn't matter. Her head is always in the clouds. The truth is, you've brought nothing but harm. I should have never talked to you at the market or brought you into the clan."

Her eyes flashed with a mix of anger and disgust. "Oh, I forgot, it was all planned"

"I'm truly sorry for deceiving you," Alex said, his voice trembling. "I needed to gain their trust. I was sent to kill you along with another Class. My technique was useful against opponents like you. I was supposed to kill you in your clan, but after working with you, I fell for you. I couldn't bring myself to do it."

Ivana's eyes blazed with fury. "Shut up! I don't care about your regrets. Every part of me wants you gone. You've endangered everyone I care about. So now, before I lose my temper, you better leave. Or the next thing you'll see is your blood splattered on that wall, and I won't care about what your mother feels."

Her voice was a whip of anger, each word cutting deeper. Alex could see the internal struggle warring within her, the pain that she tried so hard to hide.

"Your majesty," he said, his voice cracking. "I'm sorry. I never meant for things to end this way."

Ivana's eyes flashed with a mix of anger and confusion. "Sorry? Is that supposed to fix everything?"

"No," Alex replied, shaking his head. "It's not supposed to fix anything. I just need you to understand that I didn't want to hurt you."

Before Alex could say more, a sudden, searing pain erupted across his skin. His body was slammed against the wall with a force that stole his breath. Blood trickled from the gashes that appeared on his skin. He looked at Ivana, her eyes cold and hollow, reflecting a fury that seemed almost otherworldly.

Ivana's aura crackled with raw power, her rage manifesting physically. Alex's dark energy surged to protect him, but it felt like a mere wisp against her overwhelming force. Each breath he took was labored, his body pressed painfully against the wall.

Ivana's gaze was unyielding, a storm of emotions that seemed to drain any remaining hope from Alex's soul. Her control was absolute, and the coldness in her eyes was more terrifying than any physical attack.

Alex gritted his teeth against the pain, trying to find the words to bridge the chasm between them. "Your majesty, please... I just need you to understand."

But Ivana's expression remained unrelenting. The room was charged with an electric tension, the air thick with unsaid words and unresolved feelings.

"Your majesty!" Alex managed to utter, his voice strained as the pressure on his body lessened slightly. "Do you know why they wanted you to marry the King of the East?"

Ivana's focus remained unyielding, her eyes locked on him with a deadly intensity. The air was thick with tension, but Alex's words seemed to catch her attention, if only momentarily.

"It's because they wanted to usher in a new breed of demon," Alex continued, his voice trembling. "Something that would reshape humanity itself."

Ivana's grip on her power faltered just enough to show a flicker of curiosity. Despite her rage, the information was too significant to ignore. She had always wondered why the forces aligned against her were so relentless, despite her own abilities and status. Why her, specifically?

"Speak!" she demanded, her voice a harsh command.

"The child," Alex explained, "will have access to the purest and darkest form of dark energy straight from the Nether. He will bypass the seven gates of limitations and bring about devastation like the world has never seen. A devil reincarnate. And you, your majesty, were supposed to usher in this evil being. When we realized that you might complicate their plans, we were sent to force you into agreement or eliminate you. I had planned to kill you to delay the emergence of this being for another century"Ivana!" Alex managed to utter, his voice strained as the pressure on his body lessened slightly.

"Do you know why they wanted you to marry the King of the East?"

Ivana's focus remained unyielding, her eyes locked on him with a deadly intensity. The air was thick with tension, but Alex's words seemed to catch her attention, if only momentarily.

"It's because they wanted to usher in a new breed of demon," Alex continued, his voice trembling. "Something that would reshape humanity itself."

Ivana's grip on her power faltered just enough to show a flicker of curiosity. Despite her rage, the information was too significant to ignore. She had always wondered why the forces aligned against her were so relentless, despite her own abilities and status. Why her, specifically?

"Speak!" she demanded, her voice a harsh command.

"The child," Alex explained, "will have access to the purest and darkest form of dark energy straight from the Nether. He will bypass the seven gates of limitations and bring about devastation like the world has never seen. A devil reincarnate. And you, your majesty, were supposed to usher in this evil being. When we realized that you might complicate their plans, we were sent to force you into agreement or eliminate you. I had planned to kill you to delay the emergence of this being for decades."

Ivana's expression hardened, but Alex's words had sparked a deeper interest. "I killed my senior, a Beta Class, because he discovered that my true purpose didn't align with our master's goals. When I had the chance to end your life, seeing how reliant your clan was on you reminded me of how I was dependent on my mother. I couldn't do it. I need you to understand that if I had seen another way, I would have taken it. I never wanted to hurt you. I need your help, your strength, because I can't stop the classes without you."

Ivana looked away, her hands clenched into fists at her sides. The internal conflict was palpable, a storm of emotions battling within her. "You don't understand, Alex. Even if I wanted to forgive you, I'm not sure I can. Every part of me screams to keep you away, to not trust you. But... Sera said you might care, and that's..."

"That's what?" Alex pressed gently, trying to keep his voice steady despite the pain.

Ivana took a deep breath, her shoulders slumping slightly. "It makes everything more confusing. It's like there's a part of me that wants to believe what you're saying, that there's something redeemable about you. But the rest of me is too angry to even consider it."

Alex stepped closer, his voice softening. "I know I don't deserve your trust. But I'm asking for a chance to prove myself. Just one more."

Ivana's eyes met his, a mix of hope and anger swirling within them. "One more chance? How do I know this isn't another deception? That you won't betray us again?"

"I can't promise that I won't make mistakes," Alex said earnestly. "But I promise I will do everything in my power to make amends, to protect you, and to earn your trust."

Ivana stood silent for a long moment, the tension in the room almost unbearable. Finally, her voice was barely above a whisper. "I don't know if I can ever fully trust you again.

But maybe... maybe I can give you a chance to show me that you've changed. For now."

A glimmer of relief crossed Alex's face. "Thank you, your majesty. I won't let you down."

Ivana sighed, a hint of humor in her voice. "And I don't need your protection. I can take care of myself."

She released the force holding him against the wall. Alex, caught off guard by the sudden change, attempted a smile. "Well, that doesn't change the fact that you needed my help back there."

Ivana's gaze turned cold again, her expression freezing any warmth Alex had hoped for. "Oh, sorry... I thought you'd forgiven me already," he said, his attempt at light-heartedness falling flat.

Ivana's eyes remained stern, and the room was filled with an awkward silence. The glimmer of hope Alex had felt was now mingled with uncertainty as he faced the reality of the conflict still simmering between them....

"Ivana!" Alex managed to utter through the pain. "Do you know why they wanted you to marry the king of the East?"

Ivana's silence was heavy with anger, her focus unwavering as if she wanted to kill him with her gaze alone.

"It's because they wanted to bring forth a new breed of demon, one that could reshape humanity," he explained, his voice strained as the crushing force eased slightly. Ivana's eyes flickered with interest, despite her rage. She had always wondered why they targeted her specifically, despite other powerful royals with similar abilities.

"Speak!" she demanded, her voice edged with desperation.

"The child born from this union would have access to the purest and darkest form of dark energy, unbound by the Seven Gates of Limitation. They wanted you to usher in this devil reincarnate," Alex said, the words tumbling out as if they were his last hope. "But when I saw how your clan depended on you, it reminded me of how I relied on my mother. I couldn't bring myself to kill you. I just need to know if you might consider another way. I need your help to stop the classes."

Ivana's gaze remained cold, her hands clenched into fists at her sides. The internal struggle was evident on her face, a tempest of emotions swirling within. "You don't understand, Alex. Even if I wanted to forgive you, I'm not sure I can. Every part of me screams to keep you away, to not trust you. But... Sera said you might care, and that's..."

"That's what?" Alex pressed, his voice trembling with a mixture of hope and fear.

Ivana took a deep breath, her shoulders sagging slightly as she grappled with her feelings. "It makes everything more confusing. Part of me wants to believe there's something redeemable about you, but the rest of me is too angry to even consider it."

Alex stepped closer, his voice softening to a pleading tone. "I know I don't deserve your trust, but I'm asking for one more chance to prove myself. Just one."

Ivana's eyes met his, a turbulent mix of hope and anger reflecting back at him. "One more chance? How do I know this isn't another deception? That you won't betray us again?"

"I can't promise that I won't make mistakes," Alex said earnestly. "But I can promise that I will do everything in my power to make amends, to protect you, and to earn your trust."

Ivana stood in silence, her gaze fixed on Alex as if trying to read his very soul. The tension in the room was palpable. Finally, she spoke, her voice barely above a whisper. "I don't know if I can ever fully trust you again. But maybe... maybe I can give you a chance to show me that you've changed. For now."

Alex nodded, a glimmer of relief in his eyes. "Thank you, your majesty. I won't let you down."

"And I don't need your protection," Ivana added with a hint of humor, almost as if she was trying to lighten the mood. "I can protect myself."

With that, she released the force that had pinned him to the wall, and Alex was momentarily caught off guard.

"Well, that doesn't change the fact that you needed my help back there," he said with a smile, though it was met with Ivana's sudden cold stare. "Oh, sorry... I thought you had forgiven me already."

"Forgiven you?" Ivana sighed, her voice carrying a dangerous edge. She walked toward him with purposeful steps, each one echoing her anger. Alex tried to compose himself, but the intensity of her approach was overwhelming. She stood directly in front of him and, without hesitation, delivered a resounding slap that made him stagger in pain. "That's for what happened to Sera, and this is for..."

Before he could react, Ivana delivered a crushing punch to his stomach. Alex crumpled to the floor, his hands clutching his stomach as if it had been twisted inside him.

"That was for kissing me the other day."

"But...?" Alex gasped, trying to catch his breath.

"But what? You want another punch?" Ivana asked, a trace of a smile creeping onto her face as she savored the moment. She couldn't kill him, but she could at least make him suffer a bit. Suddenly, she burst into laughter, the tension in the room dissipating as her amusement took over.

Alex, still on the floor and growling in pain, looked up at her.

"Alright, I still haven't forgiven you," she said, her tone shifting back to seriousness.

"What?" Alex replied, stunned. "After all this torture?"

Ivana smiled grimly. "Oh, no, that was all for Sera and the other day. I haven't punished you for tricking me."

Alex's eyes widened in shock.

"So now, if I punish you at once, you might die. So..." Ivana said slowly, turning back toward the window with a smile. "You'll have to come back to the clan, and I will punish you there."

"Back there? I know it will be worse, so just punish me here," Alex pleaded.

"I don't want your mother to hear your screams while I torture you," Ivana said, her tone both mocking and serious. She enjoyed seeing him so confused, but Alex was still wary of her unpredictable nature.

"What if I don't want to go back?" he asked.

Ivana sighed, approaching him with a look of finality. "You think your opinion matters to me? As far as I'm concerned, by tomorrow, you pack, and we are going back."

"But I just came back."

She looked at him with an unyielding expression. It was clear to Alex that her mind was made up.

"Fine," he growled, resigned to his fate.

"That's a good boy," Ivana replied with a satisfied smile.

"Food is ready," a voice echoed from the door. Mia entered, taking in the awkward scene of Alex kneeling before Ivana. She raised an eyebrow at the sight.

"Oh, sorry," Mia said with a smirk. "I interrupted whatever this is." Alex could sense the gleam in Mia's eyes—she was definitely going to spread the word.

"Mia!" Alex yelled, rising to chase after her.

"Hey, did I ask you to leave?" Ivana commanded, freezing him in his tracks.

"But she'll tell everyone."

"Do I look like I care?" Ivana retorted.

"But..."

"..."

"Alright, I'll stay," Alex said begrudgingly.

Ivana watched him for a moment, her expression softening slightly. "You are really annoying," she said, though her words carried a hint of affection. It was the closest she could get to expressing her feelings. "Thank you, for everything."

Alex stood there, struggling to find the right response. Seeing his conflicted expression, Ivana gestured for him to leave. He hesitated, then finally smiled, his eyes showing a glimmer of hope.

"I love you too."

Ivana's eyes widened in shock, and she quickly tried to hide the blush spreading across her cheeks. "Do you want to die?"

"You won't kill me because you like me," Alex teased playfully before he dashed out of the room, trying to avoid her wrath.

"Alex!" Ivana yelled after him, the mix of frustration and lingering affection clear in her voice.

As the days passed, Alex dedicated himself to making amends with Ivana. He worked tirelessly to earn back her trust, showing through his actions that he was committed to finding a solution to stop the Classes. Every effort he made was met with skepticism from Ivana, but he persisted, determined to prove his sincerity.

Ivana, meanwhile, was preoccupied with the looming threat. The Classes' plans to create a powerful new demon were troubling, and the weight of this potential catastrophe weighed heavily on her. Despite her internal conflict and lingering anger towards Alex, she knew she needed his knowledge and skills to thwart the Classes' scheme.

Watching Alex play and goof around with his younger sister and Sera, Ivana saw how these two individuals, both annoying in their own ways, had brought about subtle changes in her life. One had been by her side since childhood, knowing her best and worst; the other, with his dark secrets and hidden agendas, was trying his best to make amends. They had shown her a glimmer of hope, making her feel she might avoid the fate of her mother.

But now, what remains is finding the enemy before they find them, first.

Epilogue

In the shadowed recesses of the dark room, a chilling silence pervaded the air, punctuated only by the faint echoes of distant battles. The remnants of the Smoke entity lay in front of him, their once formidable Gamma now nothing more than shattered echoes of his former selves, just dust. The Master remained unmoved. Alex was never the problem, his technique was.

He sat at the center of a swirling vortex of dark energy, his presence radiating an oppressive force that seemed to warp the very fabric of space around him. His eyes, twin mysteries of unyielding darkness, surveyed the clear defeat by Ivana again with a detached satisfaction. The entities, once his loyal instruments of chaos, had fallen. Because of their foolishness, not everyone can contend with someone like the Ivanas.

With a voice that resonated through the entire room, the Master spoke, his tone both commanding and cold. "Summon an Alpha," he declared, each word dripping with authority.

"It is time they understand the true power of the Nether."